THE SECRET OF THE RED SCARF

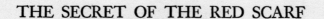

KAY TRACEY
MYSTERY STORIES

BY FRANCES K. JUDD

The masqueraders stared at one another in amazement.

A Kay Tracey Mystery

THE SECRET OF
THE RED SCARF

Frances K. Judd

GARDEN CITY BOOKS

Garden City, New York

CONTENTS

CONTENTS

CHAPTER I

A MYSTERIOUS CAR

"THE SCARF IS gorgeous!"

Wilma Worth stood looking over the shoulder of Kay Tracey in the Art Room of Carmont High School. The attractive chestnut-haired girl had just completed stencilling a bright red silk square with an intricate design of birds and flowers.

"Are you going to wear it to the masquerade?" Wilma asked.

"Yes, I am," Kay replied.

She held up a magazine and pointed to the cover. On it was pictured a lovely girl dressed in a gay Romany costume.

"I copied the design for my scarf from the one this model's wearing—in fact, when I saw the picture, it gave me the idea of masquerading as a gypsy."

"Will you tell fortunes?" Wilma teased.

"That would be too tame for Kay," said another girl, who was standing at a nearby easel.

She was Betty Worth, Wilma's twin. The two girls neither looked alike nor had similar dispositions. Betty was blond and vivacious, her sister dark-haired and dreamy looking.

"Oh I don't know," Wilma said, a faraway expression

in her eyes. "Telling the future is like having a preview of something."

"Kay," said the more practical Betty, "you ought to go dressed as a sleuth and carry a magnifying glass."

Kay laughed merrily, her brown eyes dancing. "Just how does a sleuth dress?"

Betty admitted she was stumped. It was easy to figure out how a male sleuth might dress, but she was undecided as to what a high school girl would wear to play the part.

"Just the same, I'm sure you'll run into some mystery at that masquerade," was Betty's opinion.

Wilma smiled. "Kay won't wait, I prophesy," she said. "The masquerade's over a week off and Kay Tracey never went five days without bumping into a mystery——"

The bell sounded and the three girls put their art work aside and started for the next class. Unnoticed by them, an unpleasant looking girl darted from an alcove in the Art Room. The thinness of her face was accentuated by a sharp nose and eyes that were rather small. She wore a continuous sneer on her lips.

"So Kay Tracey's going to the masquerade as a gypsy," Ethel Eaton mused. A gleam of malicious mischief came into her eyes. "Well, I'll just spike that for her!"

Ethel was intensely jealous of the popular Kay and the Worth twins. At times Ethel fancied herself to be as clever a detective as Kay, and had upon several occasions nearly ruined plans which Kay had made for solving mysteries.

As Ethel walked down the hall, the other three girls ahead of her were still discussing what they would wear to the masquerade.

"You'll look lovely as a shepherdess," Kay said to Wilma. "You might win one of the prizes."

"I hear there are to be several awards, plus a grand prize," said Betty.

"Do you know what it is?" Wilma asked.

Betty said the first prize was to be two tickets for a five-day cruise. This announcement had made the charity masquerade a sellout. A large number of people of all ages from Carmont and also the small suburb of Brantwood where the girls lived planned to attend.

"What are you going to wear, Betty?" Kay asked.

Wilma answered for her. "If there's a prize for a girl whose boy's costume fools everybody, Betty will get it. She's wearing a green habit and will be one of Robin Hood's merry men."

"You can do it with that slim figure of yours, Betty," Kay remarked with a smile.

The girls entered English class and thoughts of the masquerade were put from their minds. But as soon as school was over, the conversation continued. Kay went back to the Art Room for her scarf, then the three started for home. Usually they commuted by train, but today Kay had borrowed a car from her cousin Bill, a young lawyer who lived with the girl and her widowed mother.

"I have an errand to do for Mother at a farmhouse out of town," Kay told the twins, as they climbed into the convertible beside her. "We'll go the long way around to Brantwood."

It was a beautiful spring day and the girls enjoyed watching the bursting buds and little rivulets running down the hillsides. Beyond the city limits of Carmont fields of winter wheat were bright green and here and there farmers could be seen at work with tractors getting ready for an early planting.

Kay stopped at a rambling ranch house to pick up a

handmade coverlet which her mother was going to sell at a church bazaar. Then the girl headed toward Brantwood.

"Let's go through the woods along the Whitestone River. I just love the woods in spring," Wilma begged.

"We'll probably get stuck in the mud," said Betty practically.

"We'll try it anyway," Kay agreed, and in a few minutes turned into the narrow woods road.

They had gone about a quarter of a mile when they noticed a mud-splattered jalopy parked facing them almost in the center of the road. To pass it, Kay would have to go far down into a ditch. As she frowned, wondering if she could make it, Betty burst out:

"That's a fine place for a person to park. Give him your horn, Kay."

The girl did sound her horn, but there was no response from the other car. "I guess no one's in it," she said, slowing down.

Kay stopped just in front of the other automobile and tooted again. Still no one came.

"I'll get out and move the car if the key's in it," said Betty, opening the door and climbing out.

She hurried forward and in a moment cried out, "There's a boy asleep in here! Wake up!" she demanded.

But the figure huddled on the seat did not awaken. Betty's heart began to thump.

"Kay! Wilma!" she shouted fearfully. "Come here quick!"

The other two girls jumped out of the convertible and ran to see what the trouble was. On the front seat lay a tall, blond-haired youth of about eighteen. He wore a tan jacket and blue corduroy trousers. His eyes were closed and he was breathing heavily.

"He's unconscious," Kay said. "Either that boy's very ill or he's been injured."

As the twins looked on in awe, Kay examined the youth's head and discovered a bad bruise at the nape of his neck. She tried a little first aid on him, but when this made no impression, the girl announced that the youth should be taken to a doctor immediately.

"Let's find out who he is," Betty suggested. "Maybe we ought to take him home."

The three girls searched the young man's pockets. They were empty. Betty next tackled the glove compartment of the car but it too was empty.

"This is the strangest thing I've ever seen," said Wilma.

"There's no question but that the poor fellow was attacked," Kay stated. "Whoever did it probably robbed him and removed all the evidence."

"Look!" Betty cried suddenly, going around to the rear of the jalopy, "even the license plates are gone."

Gently the three girls lifted the unconscious form to the rear seat of Bill's convertible. Betty, having discovered that the key was still in the ignition lock of the jalopy, moved the car out of the way. Then she jumped in beside Wilma and Kay drove off.

"Are you going to take him to a doctor or the hospital?" Wilma asked.

"I've decided to take him to my house," Kay replied.

"Your house? Why?" the twins asked together.

Kay said she felt sure there was more to this than just the necessity of bringing the youth out of his unconscious state. He looked so young and pathetic she had a great desire to help him. Then she blushed self-consciously.

"There I go again, wanting to solve a mystery. But anyway, my house is closer than either a doctor or the hospital."

They reached it in a few minutes and carried the young man inside. Mrs. Tracey, Kay's pretty, sweet-faced mother, came down the stairs at once and looked at her daughter questioningly. Quickly Kay explained and then dashed to the telephone to call Dr. Rolfe.

Mrs. Tracey did not wait for the physician's arrival before working on the patient herself. She immediately went for a first-aid kit and began to administer to the youth on the sofa. But her efforts to restore him to consciousness failed also.

"Here comes the doctor," said Wilma, who was looking out a front window.

The physician hurried into the house and began his work at once. Mrs. Tracey and the girls were fascinated by his manipulations on the youth's neck and back as well as the pungent restorative which he held to the nostrils of the patient. In a few moments the young man's eyelids flickered and a few seconds later he opened his eyes wide. They were brown like her own, Kay noticed, and had a frank, honest expression. He stared first at the doctor and then at Mrs. Tracey.

"Take it easy, son," the doctor advised kindly. "You'll be all right in a little while."

The youth did not reply. His eyes wandered first to Wilma, then to Betty, and a puzzled frown crossed his face. He closed his eyes for nearly a minute, while the onlookers stood by silently.

When he opened them again, the boy turned his head slightly, so that he was looking directly at Kay, whom he had not noticed before. Suddenly he raised up on the couch, smiled broadly, and reached out his arms toward the girl.

"Sis! Sis!" he cried. "At last I've found you!"

CHAPTER II

A HAZY PAST

THE GROUP standing around the mysterious young man was dumfounded that he had mistaken Kay Tracey for his sister. Embarrassed, the girl stepped forward and seated herself beside him on the couch.

"Do I look like your sister?" she asked gently.

"You—you are my sister," the youth cried.

"I'm afraid not," Kay replied. "I take it you haven't seen your sister for some time?"

"I—no—yes—I don't know," the youth said, holding his fingers to his forehead in confusion.

Doctor Rolfe laid his hand on Kay's shoulder and indicated that she had better not talk about the subject any more.

"I think our patient should be put to bed," he said. "It would be best if he were not disturbed too much. I'll call an ambulance."

With this announcement, a wild look came into the young man's eyes. "Oh no, please!" he begged. "I want to stay here. I have plenty of money. I can pay whatever is necessary."

"But this is a private home," the doctor told him. He exchanged places with Kay. Smiling at the patient on the sofa, he said, "Now if you'll just give me your name and address——"

"Certainly. My name is——"

A look of complete bewilderment came over the face of the injured young man. He stared out the window, mumbled to himself and then turned eyes of fear to those around him.

"I don't know who I am!" he said wildly. "I can't remember."

"Do you recall where you live?" the doctor asked.

The youth closed his eyes and tried to think. A few seconds later, he opened them. They were watery and he made no pretense of trying to hold back the tears.

"Oh, what has happened to me?" he sobbed. "I don't know where I came from. Please help me remember." He felt in his empty pockets. "Did you take my papers?"

Kay now told the youth how the girls had found him unconscious in his jalopy. All traces of identification, including the license plates, had been removed. She turned to her mother.

"I'm sure our visitor will feel better after he sleeps awhile and has some food," she said. "Mother, shall we give him the guest room?"

Mrs. Tracey smiled and nodded.

"You are kind, very kind," the youth said. "I will make it up to you, I promise."

Without warning, he fell into a deep sleep. The girls were fearful that he had become unconscious again but Doctor Rolfe explained that it was merely another period of exhaustion.

"But this is a deep, natural sleep," he said. "I hope that when the young man wakes up, he will be able to explain who he is and what happened to him."

Mrs. Tracey hurried up the stairs and prepared a bed

for their unexpected patient. The others carefully carried him up the steps, then the girls left the visitor with Dr. Rolfe. The physician undressed him and put a pair of Cousin Bill's pajamas on the boy. When at last the doctor came from the room he said to the Traceys:

"I'm afraid you may have wished more on yourselves than you bargained for."

"What do you mean?" Kay's mother asked.

"This boy may be suffering from amnesia," the physician replied. "There's no telling how long it will be before his memory is restored."

A look of motherly kindness and understanding came over Mrs. Tracey's face. "I'll be very glad to take care of him. Poor boy!"

"And in the meantime I'll do everything I can to find out who he is," Kay spoke up.

"I advise you to get in touch with the police," Dr. Rolfe said. "If the young man was attacked, it is a case for them."

"All right," Kay agreed, and went at once to the telephone.

In a little while a young officer named Jackson came to the house. Since the patient was still in a deep slumber, the officer merely looked at him and then wrote down what Kay told him about the affair. The twins had left for home so he was not able to question them but Kay's story seemed to be complete. At the end of it he asked her if she would accompany him to where the jalopy was standing.

"Yes, certainly," the girl agreed. "I do hope you can find something to identify our visitor."

But an inspection by him of the old jalopy brought no results. The officer made a more thorough investigation than the girls had by pulling up the seat cushions and looking under the rubber mat which covered the floor. Finally he raised the hood of the car to look at the engine number. In a moment he whistled.

"The guy who knocked that young fellow out sure made a good job of covering his tracks," Jackson stated. "He has scratched up the engine number so nobody could possibly read it."

"You can etch it with acid and find out," Kay said.

"Yes, miss, but our department isn't equipped to do that. We'll have to send this car to the city and that'll take time."

Kay thought the inspection was over, but the police officer took out a pad and pencil and copied down the numbers on each of the four tires.

"This is our only chance for quick action," he said. "We may be able to trace the district where the young man came from. I'll ask the tire manufacturers to what points these particular numbers were sent."

"Good!" Kay exclaimed, "and will you broadcast a missing person's alarm?"

"Correct, Miss Tracey. You're right on the ball. The chief'll sign you up any time you like."

Officer Jackson grinned and said he'd have the jalopy driven to headquarters. Kay waved good-by and started back. As she entered her house, the girl met her mother coming down the stairway.

"How is he?" Kay asked eagerly.

Mrs. Tracey said that he was still asleep, but he was breathing easily and she had high hopes that when he awakened he would be able to remember who he was.

"Would you stay upstairs near him while I get dinner?" Mrs. Tracey asked her daughter.

"Certainly, Mother."

Kay hurried to the second floor and peered into the

guest room where the mysterious visitor lay asleep. Then she went in to her own room, thinking that she would start her school homework.

As she unpacked her books, Kay noticed the beautiful red scarf which was in an envelope tucked between two of them. She shook it out and had just tied it around her neck, when she heard the youth in the next room cough.

"Perhaps he's awake," she thought excitedly. "Now maybe I'll be able to find out who he is."

The patient was indeed awake. His eyes were on the ceiling and his head was moving from side to side. Hearing the girl, he turned and looked at her. Then, sitting bolt upright, he pointed at her and exclaimed:

"That scarf! Where did you get it? It's Helene's!"

Kay stood stock-still. After recovering from her surprise, she asked, "Is Helene your sister?"

"Yes, yes!"

"And what is your name?" Kay flung at him, hoping to take him by surprise so that if his memory had not yet been completely restored he would be shocked into remembering.

"My name? Why my name is—" Again a look of despair came over the youth's face. He hung his head and replied, "I don't know."

"Well, we have a good clue to finding out," said Kay happily. "I'll show you something."

She disappeared into the hall and hurried to her bedroom. There she took the magazine cover from a drawer and hurried back to the patient. Holding it up, she said:

"Is this your sister?"

"Yes, that's Helene, but she looks older," he replied.

"She's lovely," Kay remarked.

"You're right," he said, "and she looks a lot like you."

"I see then why you mistook me for your sister," Kay

said. She smiled at the young man, then asked abruptly, "Helene what?"

The pale youth wrinkled his forehead as if he were thinking very hard. After a few seconds he shook his head.

"It's no use," he said sadly. "I just don't remember anything."

Kay now told him what the doctor had said—that with good rest and food he would probably recall past events very soon.

The boy remarked that in the meantime he should have some kind of a name. What would Kay like to call him?

The girl pondered a moment, then chuckled. "How would you like to be my temporary brother?" she asked. "Suppose I call you Bro."

"Perfect." The youth smiled.

The little note of cheerfulness seemed to relieve his mind, and when Kay offered to write to the magazine and find out who the model on the cover was he actually laughed.

"You're just like a detective," he said.

Kay brought her writing kit to his room and read aloud as she wrote. As she was addressing the envelope, her mother walked into the room carrying a tray with a delicious dinner on it.

"For you, young man," she said.

"We've decided to call him Bro," Kay smiled.

"That's very appropriate," her mother agreed.

Mrs. Tracey had prepared roast beef, mashed potatoes, a green salad, ice cream, and a pot of steaming cocoa for him.

"Boy, that looks good!" he exclaimed. "Thank you, Mrs. Tracey."

"I hope you enjoy it," she said kindly.

Mrs. Tracey set the tray down on his bed and started to hurry out.

"Please come back and talk to me," Bro called. He liked this motherly person immensely and her presence seemed warm and comforting to him.

Kay said she would run to the mailbox on the corner and send the important letter while her mother talked with Bro.

As Kay hurried along the street, her heart was beating elatedly. Within a couple of days the mystery might be solved!

She dropped the air mail special delivery letter into the box, then turned back home. Some three hundred feet from her house, she saw a man run down the porch steps and hurry off.

"I wonder who he is?" she thought.

The man was too far away to be identified and as she walked up the steps the girl concluded he had been there delivering a package. As she opened the front door, however, Kay saw an envelope addressed to herself lying on the rug. The man must have shoved it under the door. Picking up the letter and opening it, Kay read with a startled gaze:

"YOUR BOARDER IS A THIEF. GET RID OF HIM AT ONCE!"

CHAPTER III

ADDRESS UNKNOWN

"What's the bad news, Kay?" asked Bill Tracey, walking into the hall from the kitchen. "You look as if you'd just inherited a million dollars—or lost it."

Bill, who was thirty years old and inclined to be a tease, had arrived shortly after Kay left to mail her letter. He was of medium height and had twinkling blue eyes. It was hard for him not to become overweight, due, he said, to Kathryn Tracey's good cooking. Though full of fun, when occasion demanded it, the lawyer could be very serious and even severe.

"Cousin Bill, this is no laughing matter," Kay said, and showed him the note.

Letters had been cut from a newspaper and pasted on a plain white sheet to form the message. There was no signature or other identification as to the sender. Kay told her cousin about the man she had seen leaving the house a few minutes before. But other than this, she had no idea who the writer might be.

"What does he mean by our boarder?" the lawyer asked.

"Oh, I forgot," Kay replied quickly, and told her cousin about the stranger who was in bed upstairs.

"Well, all I can say is you certainly get first prize for stumbling into queer situations," the lawyer remarked, as he bounded up the steps.

Kay was right on his heels and reached the doorway of the sick man's bedroom at the same moment her cousin did. She introduced him and said that Bill Tracey was a far better lawyer than she was a detective. He no doubt would have several suggestions on how to help Bro.

After a few moments it became evident that Bill Tracey also liked their visitor. Not a word was said about the note and it was not until the three Traceys had gathered at the dinner table that Kay told her mother of the warning.

"Gracious!" Mrs. Tracey exclaimed. "This sheds a whole new light on things. It may not be safe for us to keep Bro here."

"Oh, Mother, you don't think he's a thief, do you?" Kay cried.

"Well," said Mrs. Tracey after a pause, "I certainly can't say he looks like one. But then I don't know how thieves look. I've read that many times they seem very innocent."

"That's absolutely true," said Bill Tracey. "Kay, I've been thinking this thing over. Even though the boy may not be a thief, you'll have to admit that this whole affair is mighty strange. Whoever knocked him out in the car and took away his identification had a sinister reason for doing so. I agree with Kathryn that we may be putting ourselves in danger by keeping the boy here."

Kay was crestfallen. Any thoughts of danger to herself or to her family were overshadowed by sympathy for the pathetic victim upstairs. Furthermore, she was intrigued with the idea of helping him find out who he was.

"The girl on the magazine cover is lovely looking,"

she defended her position. "Chances are her brother is fine, too. Will you both do something for me?"

"What is it?" her mother said.

Kay begged that they permit Bro to stay with them at least until she had a reply from the magazine. It would not take long to reunite brother and sister and then all the Traceys' worries would be over.

The young sleuth finally had her way, although none of the Traceys slept very well that night. Each one felt it his duty to keep more or less awake and listen for any movement on the part of their strange visitor.

Bro in turn slept better than any of the others and insisted upon getting up the next morning. He came downstairs and helped Mrs. Tracey with the breakfast. The youth proved to be a master at scrambling eggs and cooking bacon and Mrs. Tracey wondered if this fact might prove to be a clue to his identity.

"Did your mother teach you to cook?" she asked him.

"My mother?" the youth asked. One of his pauses and faraway looks were the result. Then he said slowly:

"I don't know. I haven't any idea."

There was such a pained expression on the youth's face that Mrs. Tracey was sorry she had asked the question. During the meal no reference was made to the mystery and he was happy and cheerful until Kay, looking suddenly at the clock and jumping up from the table said:

"I'll be late for dear old Carmont High if I don't push off."

"Carmont?" the youth murmured, his sad look returning. "It seems to me that was where I was going when——" the sentence trailed off to nothing.

"Really?" Kay said excitedly. "Then maybe that's where your sister is. I'll keep my eyes open."

As the girl reached the hall to get her coat and books,

the telephone rang. Answering it, she found the caller to be policeman Jackson.

"I thought you'd like to know what we found out about the tires," he said.

"Oh, yes. Was it a good clue?"

"I'm afraid not," the officer answered. "Each tire was bought in a different part of the United States and none of the places was anywhere near here. No telling where that boy came from."

Kay sighed and after a little more conversation hung up. She said good-by to her mother, Bill and Bro and dashed from the house. She had to run almost all the way to the Brantwood station to make her train.

Wilma and Betty stood on the platform of the third coach, waving frantically. When the three finally flopped down into facing seats, the twins asked what the latest news was on the mystery.

"Well, my new found brother is feeling much better," Kay dimpled. "But he can't remember any more than he could yesterday."

The three girls were so busy chatting that they did not notice the approach of Ethel Eaton, who happened to be looking for a seat just at the moment Kay made her surprising remark. She paused at a little distance and drank in every word that was being said. Then she moved off down the aisle.

"Well!" she said to herself smugly.

That day it was hard for Kay to keep her mind on her studies. If she had not been such an excellent student and able to study quickly and intelligently, she probably would have flunked two quizzes that were given without warning. As it was, Kay felt she should have done better.

When she and the twins reached Brantwood again that afternoon, the Worths insisted upon going to Kay's home and calling on Bro. It was while Betty and Wilma were talking to him in the guest room that a telegram came for Kay from one of the magazine editors.

YOUR UNUSUAL LETTER RECEIVED. MODEL ON COVER HELENE BARBARA CALDWELL. HER ADDRESS UN-KNOWN. SUGGEST YOU CONTACT ARTIST JAMES BRANDON CHICAGO.

Racing upstairs with the telegram in her hand, Kay ran into the room.

"The mystery is solved!" she cried gaily. "Your sister's name is Helene Barbara Caldwell!"

The elation Kay felt was not shared by the young man. He looked at her vacantly for a few seconds and said sadly:

"My sister's name was not Helene Barbara Caldwell."

There was silence in the room for nearly half a minute. The disappointment everyone felt was keen. Kay was the first to snap out of it, referring hopefully to the second part of the telegram.

"I'll get in touch with this James Brandon right away," she said. "Your sister may be using an assumed name as a model."

Bro brightened. "Yes, please do that," he said. "Oh, not being able to remember is a horrible thing. I hope it never happens to any of you."

"You'll soon be over it," Betty said cheerfully.

Kay had already left the room. Going to her mother's bedside telephone, she asked information for the number of the artist James Brandon in Chicago. It seemed like an interminable wait, but finally a man answered. Upon learning he was Mr. Brandon, Kay introduced herself and told a little of the mystery which she was trying to solve.

"I'm sorry," the artist said, "but I never knew the model by any name but Helene Barbara Caldwell. I may be able to help you a bit, however. She was attending an art school in Carmont when I painted her. I'm sure the school can tell you about her."

Kay thanked Mr. Brandon and hung up. Her spirits were soaring again!

Before returning to the guest room, she put in a call to the Carmont Art School. To her disappointment, no one answered the phone.

"I guess everyone has gone for the day," Kay told herself. "I'll run over there myself during lunch hour tomorrow."

She returned to the room and told her latest findings. Bro became excited. Now he was sure the reason he had been on his way to Carmont was because his sister was a student at the Art School there. Perhaps he would see her the very next day!

The following morning it was difficult for Kay not to take time from classes to telephone the Art School. But between her work and an unpleasant episode which came up she found no chance.

During assembly Kay had noticed that many students were staring at her. Later, while walking from one classroom to another, the girl became even more conscious of this. Many seemed to be holding whispered conversations behind her back. Finally she spoke to Wilma about it.

"I don't know what's the matter," the dark-haired girl said, "but maybe Betty does."

Try as she might, Kay could not help wondering what the whispers were about. She grew somewhat fidgety sitting in math class as all sorts of thoughts raced through her active brain.

"Why is everyone talking about me?" she thought. "My clothes? No, they're all right."

When Kay could not think of any possible answer to do with herself personally, it occurred to her that perhaps they were not talking about her at all. Maybe someone had found out about Bro's being at her home and this was the reason. If so, what were they saying about him?

It was not until the girls met outside the chemistry lab that the truth came out. Betty, her eyes flashing, dashed up to Kay.

"Somebody has been circulating a horrible story about you!" she said indignantly. "People are saying that you have a crazy brother—that he was in some institution but you Traceys never let on that he existed. Now suddenly he's come home and you don't know what to do about it!"

CHAPTER IV

A CRUEL JOKE

"What a dreadful thing to say!" was Wilma's shocked response to Betty's announcement. "The idea! Everyone knows you're the kindest girl in Carmont High School. If you had a brother who was sort of—well, retarded, you'd be the last one to keep it a secret and try to pretend he didn't exist."

Kay herself, too shocked to speak, stood staring ahead.

"I agree with Wilma," said Betty, stamping her foot in the corridor. "And do you know what I think? I'm sure Ethel Eaton's in back of this!"

Kay, having recovered her wits, advised Betty to be very certain of this before accusing Ethel Eaton. After a pause, she added suddenly, "Girls, I have an idea!"

"Tell us what it is. The sooner we punish Ethel the better," Betty remarked.

"Oh this has nothing to do with Ethel. At least, not directly," Kay replied. "I was just thinking of poor Bro. Maybe this would be a good way to protect him."

"What on earth are you talking about?" Betty insisted impatiently.

Kay reminded the twins of the mysterious person who had knocked Bro out in his jalopy. Then there had been the threatening note left at the Tracey door.

"Don't you see how we could work this scheme?" Kay asked, her eyes sparkling. "If Bro's enemy could be made to think he has left our house, then the man wouldn't bother us again."

"A fine idea if you can work it," said Betty. "But if Bro is there, how can you make anybody think he has left?"

Kay chuckled. "By letting Ethel's story stand that a long-missing brother of mine has come home and there's no other boy at my house. Girls, I think I'm going to keep my new brother, at least temporarily."

Wilma's eyes took on a dreamy look. Then she said softly:

> *"Brother o' mine,*
> *Gone for years untold*
> *Joyfully we welcome you*
> *Into the family fold."*

"Oh, that's horrible!" Betty remonstrated. "I only hope you're the poet—but of course it couldn't be anyone else's."

Wilma did not deign to answer. By this time the three girls had entered the chemistry lab where each of them would spend the next period experimenting. While they were putting their books on the window sill, Betty whispered to Kay:

"Just because you're going to keep your new 'brother' isn't going to prevent *me* from getting square with Ethel Eaton. I just remembered how I heard the story about Bro, and it proves Ethel is guilty. Helen Winter got it from Harry Blackstone. He's Ethel's latest flame. I hear he's taking her to the masquerade and that gives me a scrumptious idea."

Just then the class bell rang and Kay hurried to her

work, saying, "Tell me later, Betty, but for goodness sake, don't do anything rash!"

Betty turned to her sister and between giggles began to explain how she planned to get even with Ethel Eaton for her malicious gossiping.

"Don't keep me in suspense," Wilma murmured as her twin paused and looked around to be sure no one else was listening.

"Well," Betty confided, "I overheard Ethel Eaton tell one of the other girls what she was going to wear to the masquerade. It's a duchess costume her mother wore years ago to some dress-up party."

"Ethel would love acting the part of a duchess," Wilma remarked. "Go on."

"Ethel mentioned that she would be sending the costume to the dry cleaner's a few days before the party. That's what gave me my brilliant idea!"

"Yes, yes. What is it?" Wilma asked eagerly.

"I'll go to the——"

At this moment Miss Sherman, the instructor, walked into the room and indicated that the girls were to go to their worktables at once. Betty walked to the far side of the room. Wilma went over and stood beside Kay.

"A note for you, Kay," Wilma said, seeing a paper lying behind a retort at Kay's place.

Wondering what it might be, Kay picked up the note and opened it. A second later she blushed.

"Why, how mean!" Wilma cried, seeing what lay before Kay.

It was a crude drawing of a girl with the initials K.T. under her. Seated beside her on the floor playing with a set of blocks was a baby. Under it was scrawled, "My brother."

"This ghastly joke has gone far enough!" Wilma said

with determination. "The minute school is over today I'm going to tend to Ethel Eaton myself!"

"No talking please, girls," Miss Sherman called out.

Kay, who had been about to answer her friend's outburst, picked up a pad and pencil and wrote on it:

"The best way to punish Ethel is to ignore her. She'll be dying to know what we thought of her drawing. Let's pretend I never received it."

As Wilma nodded and started her experiment, Kay tucked the paper into her shirt pocket. She found it difficult to keep her mind on her work. The tender hearted girl was incensed by Ethel's move and felt doubly sorry that the poor stranger at the Tracey home had to be subjected to such gossip. More than ever Kay wanted to help him and could hardly wait for the lunch hour to arrive so she might hurry over to the Art School and learn what she could about his sister.

"Can I help you, Miss Tracey?" a voice over her shoulder asked. "You seem to be having trouble getting started this morning."

Kay turned and smiled. "Oh thank you, Miss Sherman," she said. "I'll begin my experiment at once. I'm sure I can do it alone."

The girl sleuth determined to settle down and put her mind on her school work. The experiment went along well for about ten minutes, then Kay's mind began to wander again.

"I must pay attention," she told herself sternly, and reached for a bottle on the shelf above.

Carefully she measured a small quantity of the liquid into a test tube. Then, without noting particularly where she was replacing the bottle, Kay set it back on the shelf some distance from where it had stood.

Wilma was carrying on a completely different experiment. She was busy boiling a fluid over a Bunsen burner and like Kay her mind had begun to wander. She too felt exceedingly sorry for the young man at the Tracey home and decided that she would work hard with Kay trying to solve the mystery.

"If Bro could only remember a little bit more," Wilma thought. "I think I'll go and talk to Dr. Rolfe myself and find out whether there's something we can do to——"

"Miss Worth," the instructor called, "the liquid in your experiment is boiling away. You'd better finish your work before it evaporates."

Wilma shook off her absent-minded mood and added a few drops of green fluid from a bottle just above her. At once the boiling liquid turned a murky shade.

"So far, so good," Wilma told herself, and consulted her chemistry book. "Now for the last part of the experiment."

Her eyes still on the book she reached up for a certain bottle. Instead of the one she thought she was taking, her fingers closed around the bottle Kay had put in the space a few minutes before.

Unfortunately Wilma did not read the label on it. After uncorking the bottle, she poured a quantity of the contents into the boiling fluid.

The next moment there was a loud explosion!

CHAPTER V

MISTAKEN IDENTITY

THE FORCE of the explosion in the high school chemistry laboratory sent Wilma and Kay reeling backward. Betty and other students in the laboratory, stunned at first by the noise, now turned and rushed forward to help the two girls. Miss Sherman ran hurriedly from her desk in the far side of the room.

"What happened?" she cried.

By this time Kay and Wilma had picked themselves up from the floor. They were ruefully surveying their appearance and the destruction around them. There was a cut on Wilma's chin and a burned spot on Kay's right arm. Pieces of broken glass were imbedded in their sweaters and skirts. The work table was littered with chemicals and broken bottles.

"Oh, Wilma—K—Kay," Betty's voice was fearful. "Are—are you all right?"

"Yes," Kay replied, recovering quickly from her temporary shock. "But this place is a wreck."

"Never mind that, so long as you're not hurt," Miss Sherman replied in relieved tones. "How do you feel, Miss Worth?"

Wilma was on the verge of tears and said that she felt

pretty shaky but had not been injured. The scratch on her chin was slight.

"You're lucky! You could have been killed!" said a boy standing nearby.

"And you might have had your eyes injured by flying glass," said another, who was known to be a doleful minded youth.

Miss Sherman asked two other boys to clean things up and requested that Kay and Wilma go with her to her office and explain what had taken place. The teacher applied an antiseptic to Wilma's scratch and some unguent to the burn on Kay's arm. Then she helped them pick the pieces of glass from their clothing.

"Now, whatever caused the explosion?" she asked, as they all sat down.

Neither of the girls could give a definite answer to this. Kay knew she had not caused the explosion but admitted she had been a little absent-minded at the time. Perhaps something she had done unwittingly had been the reason. Wilma in turn knew only that she had poured some fluid into the boiling liquid and then *poof!*

"Do you girls always read the labels on the bottles carefully before you open them?" Miss Sherman questioned.

Suddenly Wilma recalled that she had not done so. "It's all my fault—I know it is," she said and burst into tears. "I—I—didn't look at the label."

The teacher, realizing the incident had been a great shock to Wilma, did not reprimand either girl severely. After gently cautioning them to exercise greater care in future experiments, Miss Sherman suggested that Wilma go home. She asked if Kay would like to go also, but the girl shook her head.

"I feel all right, really I do," she assured the teacher.

"But I'm sure I had something to do with the explosion —maybe I set one of the bottles back in the wrong place and Wilma picked it up. I'll gladly pay for my share of the damage."

"I will, too," Wilma sobbed. "Oh, Kay! To think I might have injured you badly for life!"

Kay put her arm around her friend and walked back to the laboratory with her. "Please don't worry any more about it," she said. "We're both all right and that's a lot to be thankful for."

By this time the boys, with the help of several girl students, had cleaned the messy section of the laboratory. The only evidence of the accident was a small scorch on the linoleum and the empty shelves. Wilma's chemistry book was completely ruined. As she looked at the remnants, she smiled through her tears, saying:

"As a poet I'm a poor chemist anyway."

Kay and Betty walked with her to the girls' locker room and then said good-by. Since there were still ten minutes left before the end of the period, Kay decided to go to the cafeteria for an early lunch. That would leave her free to make the trip to the art school during the noon hour.

Kay made good time and reached the school at five minutes past twelve. She inquired at the desk for Helene Barbara Caldwell.

The woman receptionist smiled. "Miss Caldwell used to be a student here. She modeled at times and went out to pose for artists in the nearby communities."

Kay was disappointed to learn that Bro's sister was no longer enrolled with the school but asked for the model's present address. To her further dismay the woman said she did not know where the girl was.

"Perhaps Helene's best friend at the school may

know," the receptionist said. "Miss Caldwell and Vicki Raponi were inseparable."

"Vicki Raponi?" Kay repeated in surprise. "You mean the daughter of Victor Raponi the art dealer?"

"Yes."

Kay thanked the woman and hurried off, elated to learn that Vicki, whom Kay knew well, was a friend of Helene's.

"I'll just have time to dash to Raponi's Art Shop before afternoon classes," she thought, glancing at her wrist watch. "If Vicki's there, she may be able to clear up the mystery."

Kay signaled an approaching bus and climbed aboard. By the time she had made change for the fare and put her money in the slot, the girl was at her destination. She had saved five precious minutes by riding.

Raponi's Art Store was well-known in the community and the pleasant Italian dealer was a friend and adviser to all the Carmont High art students. As Kay opened the door and walked toward the rear of the shop, she could see Mr. Raponi looking at a picture on the counter. He glanced up and gave a little start.

"Helene! My dear Helene! You have returned to us!"

Kay was amazed. Again she had been mistaken for Helene Caldwell!

"I'm afraid you've made a mistake, Mr. Raponi," Kay said to the art dealer. "Don't you recognize me—I'm Kay Tracey."

The man stared at her. Then he apologized, saying, "But of course—I am very sorry, Miss Tracey. The light is so dim in my store. They tell me I should get better fixtures. More money! More money! That is what everything is today. I cannot afford to fix up my shop and still sell my pictures and supplies cheap. Then the students at the art school—what would they do? So—again—I am so sorry I think you are my daughter's friend Helene Caldwell."

"That's all right," Kay replied. "It is because of Helene I'm here."

It was the art dealer's turn to look surprised. "Helene was staying with my Victoria for several weeks," he said. "But she went away very suddenly. I think it was because of some man she did not like—he telephoned her and said he was coming here."

"Do you know where she went?" Kay asked.

"No, I have no idea."

"Does your daughter Vicki know?"

The art dealer shrugged, saying possibly she did. But if so, she had failed to tell him.

"Where can I get in touch with Vicki?" Kay questioned him.

"She is at Lake Valentine at a—what you call it—a party house." The man laughed. "I mean, house party. Do not ask me where the place is. Victoria told me the name, but I forget." The man waved his arms excitedly. "She said she would let me know when she arrived. But I have not heard from her. Maybe a letter takes a long time to get here. Well, Miss Tracey, I think that is all I can tell you."

Kay thanked him and hurried away.

"I'll drive to Lake Valentine tomorrow," Kay told herself as she entered the school building. "Lucky today's Friday."

Upon reaching home that afternoon, she was delighted to see her mother and Bro seated in the sun on the front porch of their house. Both were reading and Kay smiled, knowing that her mother was trying by this method to restore their visitor's memory. Bro and Mrs. Tracey looked up and greeted the girl.

"Any news for me?" Bro asked her quickly.

Kay, bubbling over with enthusiasm, sat down beside him and told what she had learned.

"If Cousin Bill can spare his car tomorrow, I'll drive to Lake Valentine and talk to Vicki Raponi. Bro, would you like to go along? I'll ask Wilma and Betty too."

"Yes, I would," the young man said eagerly.

Cousin Bill was glad to lend Kay his convertible and the following morning the four young people set off. Kay had telephoned Mr. Raponi for further news but he still had received no word from his daughter.

"We'll have to do some real sleuthing," Kay told the others. "Lake Valentine is a fairly large place and I have no idea where Vicki is staying."

"That's like looking for a needle in a haystack," Wilma said dubiously.

"And I hope it won't stick us if we find it," Betty added.

Upon reaching the town of West Grove at the foot of the lake where there was a dam and waterfall, Kay went at once to the post office to inquire for Victoria Raponi. The clerk said he had never heard of her. Disappointed, Kay next tried a drugstore. Again, she had no success.

"Any suggestions?" she asked, coming back to the car and relating her failure.

"Why don't we just drive around the lake to see if any place looks as if it were having a house party?" Bro spoke up.

"All right," Kay agreed, climbing in behind the wheel.

She started off, taking the north side of the lake first. They traveled the whole two miles of its length without seeing any place where a group of young people were in evidence.

"We've probably come on a wild goose chase," Wilma sighed.

Kay did not reply for she had just turned up the south side of Lake Valentine and was looking intently into the distance. She had caught sight of a number of young men and women crowding around a dock.

"I believe we're in luck," she said.

Putting on more speed, Kay drove up to the group and stopped. She hopped from the car and ran toward the dock. Vicki Raponi was there. But to Kay's amazement she was sobbing as if her heart would break. Two of her friends were trying to comfort her.

Kay touched the arm of a youth at the edge of the circle and asked him what was the matter. He replied excitedly that they thought a girl and a youth had drowned. She was a special friend of Vicki Raponi.

Kay's heart began to pound in sudden fear, as she pushed her way through the group of young people in order to reach Vicki.

The weeping girl turned. "Oh, Kay, something dreadful has happened! I—I'm so afraid—my best friend—overturned in a canoe and was——" Vicki choked and could not go on.

Kay took hold of the girl's hand. "I'm terribly sorry. Can I do anything?" As Vicki merely started weeping again, Kay asked gently, "What is your friend's name?"

Vicki's sorrowful reply was, "Helene Caldwell."

CHAPTER VI

A HOAX

"MY SISTER—drowned! Oh no!"

The cry came from Bro, who had stepped from the car and joined the group behind Kay.

"Your sister?" several in the group repeated.

Vicki Raponi turned questioning eyes on the youth. "Your sister? I didn't know Helene had a brother," she said perplexed.

Quickly Kay explained why she and Bro were there, but refrained from telling Vicki they did not know what the youth's right name was. She merely said he was trying to find his sister. Certain clues seemed to lead to the girl about whom Vicki was now so worried.

"Are you sure that it was Helene in the upset canoe?" Kay asked.

"Well it seems as if it must have been," Vicki answered.

She explained that a farmer had phoned saying he lived down the road and had seen the accident. A girl and a young man had let their canoe be swept over the falls at the end of the lake. The craft had overturned and that was the last he had seen them. The farmer was sure that they had drowned. He also was sure of having seen them at the cottage the day before.

"How long ago was this?" Kay questioned quickly.

"Oh, half an hour."

"We were down at that end of the lake just about at that time," Kay said. "We didn't see anything unusual."

"That's right," said Betty, who had joined the excited group.

"Then maybe—maybe the report is false," Bro spoke up hopefully.

Kay asked who the farmer was and was told he had not given his name. The girl thought this was very strange and since Helene seemed to be a mysterious person, the report might indeed be false. But why had it been given? And who was the person who had telephoned? Kay took Vicki aside and repeated what Mr. Raponi had said about Helene and that he thought she had run away to avoid the attentions of a man she did not like.

"That's true," Vicki said. "And I don't like Tad Bacon either. He was in the canoe with her. He's a sneaky person. And to think he had to show up here when Helene thought she was safely hidden."

"Why did she bother with him?" Kay asked.

"He seems to hypnotize her," Vicki replied. "I don't think Helene knows him well. He showed up at the Art School with a letter of introduction, Helene said."

Vicki told how he had crashed the house party unexpectedly and had talked Helene into letting him stay.

"What does Tad look like?" Kay asked.

"Average height. But his long, thin face gives me the creeps."

As Kay made a mental note of this, Vicki continued:

"I tried to warn Helene against being friendly with him, but she paid no attention. This morning they went off in the canoe and that was the last we saw of them. Oh, I hope they didn't drown!"

"Tell me why you don't like Tad Bacon," Kay asked, becoming more suspicious of him by the minute.

"It's hard to explain," Vicki said. "He just doesn't seem like an honest person."

Kay was very much worried that Tad Bacon, instead of being a friend was an enemy of Helene's and Bro's, assuming of course that Helene was the youth's sister. She had not forgotten that Bro had indicated he had lots of money. Was Bacon trying to steal a family fortune perhaps?

"Oh dear," Kay thought. "Each clue I track down only seems to make the whole situation worse."

Feeling that she must not reveal this to Bro, Kay managed a smile as she walked toward him and said:

"I'm sure Helene is alive. Now we must find out where she is and bring her back here."

At Vicki's suggestion a couple of the boys set off in a canoe to make a search of the lake. As the girls watched them paddle away, a colored maid came hurrying out of the cottage where the group were standing.

"Miss Vicki Raponi! Miss Vicki!" she called. "Telephone for you."

"Oh, maybe it's Helene!" Bro cried eagerly.

He, Kay and the twins followed Vicki to the cottage. They stood by expectantly as she picked up the telephone. A moment later they heard her joyous shout.

"Helene! You're alive! Thank goodness! We thought you had drowned."

"Let me speak to her!" Bro pleaded.

But Kay held him back, reminding the youth that this girl might not be his sister after all.

"Better let Vicki find out," she advised.

There was a long pause as Vicki listened intently to what her friend was saying. While waiting Bro walked up and down the room agitatedly. Twice he started for the phone, then thought better of it and stalked away.

Finally Vicki spoke. "I'm terribly sorry, Helene," she said. "But please come back here or else to my home in Carmont. Don't run away again. Please!"

Kay, Bro and the twins looked startled. Helene was not coming back!

"Wait! I want to tell you something important," Vicki went on. "Helene, listen. There are some people here to see you. One of them says he's your—Helene, wait! Please!"

Vicki hung up, sagging against the table on which the telephone stood. Turning around, she said:

"Helene wouldn't wait. She's gone away again. She wouldn't tell me where. Oh, I tried my best——"

Tears came to Vicki's eyes. Kay went forward and patted her arm. "You did all you could. Don't worry. We'll find Helene somehow."

Vicki shook her head. She did not think so. Helene had told her Tad Bacon had revealed some news to her, so that it would be impossible for the girl ever to see her family or friends again. Helene was saying a final good-by, although Tad had advised her not to get in touch with anyone. He had said he would take care of this.

"So he phoned calling himself a farmer!" Kay thought.

As Vicki finished her story, there was complete silence in the room. The young people looked at one another in utter amazement and Bro collapsed on the couch. Kay at once went to sit beside him, trying to bolster up the boy's spirits.

Wilma asked for a glass of cool water for him. After drinking it, the youth revived a bit, then asked that he be taken home.

"But first tell them about me, Kay," he suggested. "Maybe somebody here can find out who I am."

Amazed, the various members of the house party listened attentively to the strange story, ending with the idea that Helene might be using an assumed last name. They were touched by Bro's pathetic plight and promised to do everything they could to help solve the mystery.

Kay suddenly had an idea. "Do I really look a lot like Helene?" she asked Vicki.

"Yes, you do," the art student replied. "At a distance you two could easily be mistaken for each other."

"This may help me find her," Kay thought.

If she could only locate Tad Bacon, maybe she could fool him into mistaking her for Helene and learn what the influence was which he held over Helene. The scheme might also help Kay find the girl herself.

"What sort of clothes did Helene like to wear?" she next asked.

"Well, when she was dressed up," Vicki said, "she loved to wear suits and little hats with veils."

"Perfect," Kay thought. "A veil would be a good way to disguise myself enough to fool Tad Bacon."

Taking Vicki aside, Kay told her of the scheme and asked what the girl thought of her chances of making it work.

"Risky," Vicki said. "But Kay Tracey could get away with it. I'd make a flop of the whole thing."

Kay asked her many questions about Helene's mannerisms and way of speaking. Ten minutes later she felt that she had a full description of the missing girl and with a little luck would be able to imitate her perfectly.

"Helene left some clothes here," Vicki said. "Would

you like to try them on and I'll tell you exactly how much you look like her?"

"Oh yes, I'd love to."

Kay explained to Bro and the twins what she was going to do and went upstairs with Vicki. While she removed her sweater and skirt, the other girl brought out a dainty white blouse and brown wool gabardine suit which belonged to Helene. Kay slipped them on. They fitted her perfectly!

Vicki now adjusted a smart toast-colored straw hat over Kay's wavy chestnut hair. She pulled down the half veil over her face and then walked across the room to survey the effect.

"Right now you look enough like Helene to be her sister, but you couldn't quite pass for Helene herself," Vicki stated. "Wait a minute! Let me fix you up a bit."

Taking out a make-up kit, she began to daub Kay's face. First she tinted her cheekbones with orange color rouge. Next she darkened the girl's eyebrows a trifle. Finally she put the slightest bit of eye shadow in the crease of Kay's chin to deepen the line.

Once more the art student walked off to look at her work. She smiled.

"It's coming! It's coming!" she cried. "One more thing and you'll look exactly like Helene."

From the pocket of her suitcase she took a pair of pearl earrings. After Kay had put them on, Vicki proclaimed that the disguise was perfect.

"I want my friends downstairs to see you," Vicki said, delighted with the results of her handiwork. "Come on. I'll bet you can fool them."

The house party group declared that they certainly would think Kay was Helene Caldwell except for the fact the missing girl could not possibly have reached the cottage in such a short time.

"Wow!" said one of the boys, whistling. "Say, star, what are you playing in now?"

Wilma turned on him. "Shush! This is serious business."

"I'm serious," he retorted. "How about a date?" he called to Kay.

"Don't give him one," Betty spoke up. "He'd probably order two sodas and drink both of them."

"Oo, a knockdown blow." He laughed. "Seriously, Kay, you certainly could pass for Helene."

"If you'll just speak a little lower and laugh a little higher, you'll fool everybody," Vicki declared.

The only person in the room who did not take kindly to this masquerade was Bro. Rising from the couch, he walked toward Kay, looking very confused. Holding his hand to his head, he cried out:

"Is this a joke on me? Are you my friend Kay or my sister Helene?"

As the others looked at him, startled, the youth suddenly realized that they thought he might have lost more than his memory. Quickly he explained that he had not seen his sister for five years. She might have changed enough to look as Kay did at this very moment.

"You haven't seen her for five years?" Kay asked, delighted that this added clue had suddenly been revealed. Perhaps Bro was beginning to get his memory back!

"That's right," Bro said excitedly. "And I remember something else, too. When I started out to find my sister, I was carrying a lot of important papers."

"Then they were stolen from you," Betty declared angrily. "The person who attacked you in the car wanted them himself."

"Or else wanted to be sure you didn't deliver them to somebody he didn't wish to have them," Kay guessed. "And as soon as I change my clothes we're going to find out who the man is!"

CHAPTER VII

KAY'S RUSE

As KAY guided the convertible smoothly along the lake road, its four passengers automatically drank in the attractive scene. On one side was the glittering blue water, on the other trees and flowering bushes in profusion. Yet their thoughts were more on the problem at hand than the loveliness around them.

"I think we ought to drive back to West Grove and make some inquiries about Helene," Kay said. "Maybe at the bus or railroad station we can pick up a clue about where she went."

"Yes, let's do that," Bro urged.

Upon reaching town, Kay parked in the public square and they all got out. Wilma and Betty offered to go in one direction while Kay and the youth investigated the other side of town.

"Let's meet here in twenty minutes," Kay suggested. "Then we'll have a bite to eat."

"Good idea," said Betty. "I'm starved."

The twins chose the east end of town where the bus station was located but learned that only a group of boys had boarded the one out-of-town bus to leave in the past hour.

"Well, we drew a blank here," Betty remarked. "Where do we go now?"

"Let's try the restaurants," Wilma suggested. "Helene and Tad might've had lunch before they left."

The twins walked up one street and down another, going into the three eating places they found. At the last, a diner, the good-natured owner seemed to be sure he had served the couple they sought. Hopeful he could give them some information, the girls ordered bowls of soup. They would eat the rest of their meal with Kay.

"Everyone gets in here sooner or later," he said as he served them. "Now this one couple, they struck me as kind of mysterious."

"Oh they must have been the ones," Wilma cried. "Did the man seem as if he was—well, hypnotizing the girl?"

"He sure did," the proprietor replied. "And she looked pretty scared—only I thought he was tryin' to get her to marry him. But I hope she never does. I didn't like him."

"Did he look like a crook?" Betty burst out.

The man laughed. "How does a crook look? I've seen 'em tall, short, fat and thin. But seriously, I wouldn't trust the guy who was in here—no sir. I can't tell you why, just a hunch."

Actually, he could give the twins no information to assist them in finding Helene and disappointed they left the diner. On the other side of town, Kay was having no better luck. The agent at the railroad station had not been able to help her and the baggage man and news-dealer could give no clues either.

"I'll try that taxi driver," Kay said to Bro presently, as she noticed a cab parked near the station.

Bro smiled. "He looks so sleepy I don't believe he would have noticed anybody."

This proved to be the case. The fellow admitted that he had had no passengers for a couple of hours and had been dozing.

Kay was puzzled as to how Helene and Tad had left town. Since neither of them had a car, they must have ridden on some kind of a conveyance. Kay concluded that if it were not a public vehicle they must have asked some farmer in the neighborhood to drive them away. She told Bro her idea, adding:

"I think the telephone company can help us out."

After asking a passerby where the building was located, she and the youth set off up the street. The woman in charge of the small exchange listened sympathetically to Kay's story. Since she was acquainted with every farmer who lived around the lake, as well as the summer residents, she personally put in calls to each one and introduced Kay to them over the wire. The fifth call brought the first ray of hope to the girl.

"Yes, a couple did come hurrying into my place from the lake, asking for a ride," he said. "They wanted to know if I would drive them over to the main bus line. It was the quickest five dollars I ever earned." He laughed.

"Did you find out where they were going?" Kay pressed quickly.

"They didn't make any bones about it. Why, did you have an idea they was trying to hide?"

Kay did not answer the question directly. She said that she was endeavoring to get an important message to the young woman and was having a hard time finding her.

"Well," drawled the farmer, "I believe they was headin' for North Newton."

"You didn't hear them mention any address in that town?" the girl asked.

"No, I didn't, miss."

"Thank you very much," Kay said. "You've helped me a lot."

She hung up and turned excitedly to Bro, telling him the news and saying she would follow the clue at once. They hurried back to meet the twins who became excited upon hearing what their friend had found out.

"Let's go right over to North Newton," Kay suggested.

"What! Without eating first?" Betty objected. "It's miles to that place. I'd be in a dead faint before I reached it if I don't eat something."

"All right, you win." Kay laughed.

The twins saw to it that she, as well as they, ate a good lunch, but none of the girls could induce Bro to eat very much. The morning's excitement had taken its toll of him and he looked very pale. As they finished, Kay said to him kindly:

"Sleuthing is a hard job, Bro, when you're not feeling strong. Will you do me a favor? Let one of the girls drive you home. The other one and I will go over to North Newton and continue our search."

The youth made a feeble remonstrance but was glad to accept the offer when Kay became insistent.

"I'll take him home," Wilma offered. "I think I've had enough sleuthing for one day."

"But, Kay, how will you and Betty get to North Newton?" Bro asked.

"The same way that couple did."

Kay suggested they all drive to the main bus route and from there Wilma and Bro could return home in the car. She and Betty would hop a bus and later return to Brantwood by train.

At two o'clock the group separated, Kay and Betty waving good-by from the express bus. A half hour's ride brought them to North Newton.

"Where do we begin hunting?" Betty asked.

"In a dress shop," Kay replied, her eyes dancing. "I have an idea."

She explained that since North Newton was a fairly large town it would be pretty difficult to find Helene Caldwell and her escort. It might take hours to get any clue.

"My plan is to have them see me," said Kay. "I'll buy some clothes just like Helene's and fix myself up so I'll resemble her enough for any acquaintance of hers to be fooled."

"You mean, that if a person speaks and calls you Helene, you may be able to find out where she's living."

"Exactly," Kay nodded.

"But where's all the money coming from?" Betty remarked. "I can't lend you any. Two dollars is the sum total of my wealth at the moment."

"Money. You're right," Kay mused. Then she had an idea. "There's a branch of Thompson's Carmont store here. Mother has an account there. I can probably charge anything I buy in this one."

"I'm sure your mother would spend thirty dollars any time to solve a mystery," Betty needled her.

Reaching Thompson's, the girls walked in and went at once to the credit department. Kay showed her driver's license and was told she might charge up to fifty dollars worth of merchandise.

She and Betty hurried to the misses' section and Kay found a brown wool gabardine suit which was almost a duplicate of the one Helene owned. Kay purchased it.

Their next stop was the blouse counter and then the millinery department. Here Kay had a little more trouble. There were no toast-colored straw hats which looked anything like the one Helene had worn.

"I guess we'll have to try some other place," Kay said finally with a sigh.

The girls visited three hat shops before they were successful. But at last Kay located an inexpensive beret-type hat with a half-face veil on it.

"It's terribly becoming," Betty remarked.

"Thanks, Betty. While I go to the powder room at Thompson's and change my clothes, will you buy me a little make-up kit like Vicki Raponi had and bring it to me?"

Back at the store once more, Betty went to the cosmetic counter. Half an hour later the two girls were on the street once again, Kay very attractive in her new get-up.

"Maybe you ought to wear outfits like this all the time," commented Betty. "The only trouble is, you look about five years older. And on second thought, I don't believe Ronald would approve of the change."

Kay laughed. "I'll just call this a masquerade costume," she said.

The two girls walked along various business streets for twenty minutes without having anyone speak to them or evince any unusual interest. Once a girl across the street waved, but before Kay could cross over to her she disappeared around a corner and could not be located.

"Maybe you'd do better alone," Betty suggested. "How about going ahead of me? I'll stay half a block behind you."

"That's not a bad idea," Kay agreed.

Betty pretended to say good-by to her friend and

walked over to look in a shop window. She became so intent in a display of attractive purses, that when she turned around, Kay was not in sight. A bit worried, Betty hurried up the block. Reaching the corner, she looked in every direction. Kay had disappeared!

Meanwhile Kay had reached the corner. Assuming that Betty was not far behind, she had turned down a side street and then into another.

Suddenly a man stepped from a store and stood still to stare at her. He had a long thin face and unfriendly eyes. Kay's heart began to thump. Was this Tad Bacon?

Stepping up to Kay, the stranger said severely, "I thought I told you to stay out of sight for a few days!"

Kay gave the high laugh in imitation of Helene Caldwell. Then she said in a voice slightly lower than her own:

"I'm sorry. Please take me home."

The man walked along beside her. Kay was fearful that she might make one wrong move. If she could keep her wits about her, she might soon come face to face with Helene Caldwell! With bold strides the stranger beside her led the way down the street and beyond the stores and houses.

"Helene must be living on the outskirts of town," Kay decided.

There was no conversation until they reached a car parked at the side of the road. Then suddenly the stranger turned, shook Kay hard by the shoulders and said:

"So you thought you could get away with this, eh? I'll fix you!"

Yanking open the rear door of the car, he unceremoniously threw the girl in ahead of him. Following her, he slammed it shut, then whipped out a handkerchief and stuffed it into her mouth. As she struggled to free herself, he took two coils of thin wire from his pockets and bound her arms and feet with it. Climbing over to the front seat, the man started the car and whizzed down the road.

CHAPTER VIII

A TRICK BACKFIRES

THE STRANGER at the wheel of the car in which Kay Tracey was a prisoner drove like a madman. As the automobile swerved around curve after curve, the girl was jolted from side to side on the rear seat. The wire bonds cut into her flesh painfully.

"Oh, where is he taking me?" Kay thought despairingly, unable to keep back the tears.

She kept wondering whether he still thought she was Helene Caldwell or whether he had guessed the truth that she was masquerading as the girl.

"In either case my stunt didn't work," Kay told herself ruefully. "And what will Betty think? She'll be frantic when I don't show up."

This last thought gave Kay a gleam of hope. No doubt Betty would report the affair to the police and a search would be started. But as the ride continued at breakneck speed, Kay realized that the farther she got from North Newton the slimmer her chances became.

She tried to figure out the route the man was taking, but with so many twists and turns she lost track of the direction. From the stillness, though, Kay was sure they were traveling deeper and deeper into farming country.

"There may be a lot of people mixed up in this mystery," she thought. "Perhaps he's taking me to their hide out. Oh, I must get free somehow!"

Kay tried to sit up but found this impossible. In the struggle she almost rolled off the seat.

A choking sensation began to take possession of her. The gag in her mouth seemed to be growing larger and Kay felt as if she could not stand it there another moment.

"If I could only loosen this handkerchief it's tied with!" she thought desperately.

Suddenly the car gave a tremendous twist and stopped abruptly. Kay was thrown violently to the floor, landing on her back.

She hit her head hard, and lost consciousness.

When Kay awoke some time later, it was pitch black around her. She had no idea where she was and for a moment thought she must be in her own bedroom. Then Kay realized she was bound and gagged. As her full senses slowly returned, the girl recalled the whole horrible adventure.

"I'm still in that kidnaper's car," she told herself. "Did we have an accident?"

There was not a sound. A frightening thought came to her. Was her kidnaper perhaps in the front of the car no longer alive? She shivered involuntarily.

"I must do something," Kay told herself.

She tried to move, and though it was painful she found that the jolting apparently had loosened her bonds a bit.

"Now if I can only get them off!" she wished hopefully.

With superhuman effort Kay pulled herself to a sitting position. The effort made her gasp and this together with the gag nauseated her.

It was several minutes before she had strength enough to renew her efforts. Then began a long struggle as she tried to get the bonds off her arms. Kay soon found out that this was hopeless and the wire around her feet was even more stubborn.

"If I could only yell!" Kay thought hopelessly.

Then a plan for getting rid of the gag came to her. She would try to rub off the handkerchief which was holding the gag in place. After brushing her cheek back and forth against the car seat for several minutes, she finally managed to make the handkerchief drop around her neck.

Then came the task of ridding herself of the gag. This proved to be impossible because her tongue, wedged tightly against the bottom of her mouth, was useless to help her.

"Something will have to pull the gag out for me," Kay decided.

She thought of the door handles and managed to twist herself around so she could reach one of them. Fortunately it was a half handle and Kay was able to insert the end of it between her lips.

At first the gag refused to move. But with persistence she finally managed to dislodge the gag. As it dropped to the floor, she heaved a sigh of relief.

"Now I can scream for help," she told herself excitedly.

But here another disappointment awaited her. When she tried to cry out, Kay could force nothing from her throat but a whisper. Her vocal cords seemed paralyzed and would be for some time, she knew. A sense of desolation overcame her but after she had rested a bit, Kay's old pluck and determination returned.

"If I can't make a sound myself, I'll have to make the horn do it for me!" she decided. "The next thing is to get myself over to the front seat."

Suddenly she recalled that a lifeless figure might be sprawled on it. In her eagerness to get free she had forgotten him. Again she shuddered.

"I'll just have to face it," she finally told herself grimly.

With every ounce of strength Kay pulled herself to her knees. Then using the rear seat of the car as a lever, she managed to stand up.

With palpitating heart she looked into the front seat. *It was empty!*

"Thank goodness!" Kay sighed in relief. "Now to get myself to that horn."

It was painful toppling herself into the front seat but she did it. Once there, Kay wriggled into a position so she could lay her head on the horn.

Its first sharp blast cut the stillness like a pistol shot and made her ears ache. But she kept on blowing the horn, nevertheless.

"Someone will certainly hear it," she told herself hopefully.

When five minutes went by and there was no response to her call, Kay was forced to stop the noise. Her ears were ringing and she felt faint. It suddenly occurred to her that along with the shock of being captured she had eaten nothing for many hours.

"I wonder what time it is," Kay mused.

When she felt better, Kay wriggled into still another position and with her teeth managed to pull out the light switch. She glanced at the car clock. It was midnight!

"I must have blacked out for a long time," Kay thought. "Poor mother! She must be worried sick. *How* am I going to get loose?"

Kay toyed with the idea of letting herself out of the car. But being unable to see the ground very well, she was fearful of dropping into water or over an embankment. It would be better to stay where she was until daylight.

Of one thing Kay was sure. She was in a very isolated spot. Not one car had passed since she had regained consciousness.

"I'm probably not even on a road," she told herself miserably. "Maybe no one will ever find me—at least not until it's too late!"

Again she struggled with her wire bonds but could not budge them. Giving up, she leaned on the horn once more.

In a moment she heard a sound which made her heart leap hopefully. It was another car horn.

Help was coming!

This time Kay tooted three blasts, then stopped. The other car also tooted three times. This kept up at intervals until the girl could hear the sound of a motor.

A few minutes later the car door was flung open and a state trooper gazed down at the girl. He whistled, then with one arm around Kay pulled her from the car to a standing position on the ground.

"What in creation's been going on?" he asked, and introduced himself as Trooper Grayson.

As he took off the wire binding Kay's arms and feet, she told her story in a whispered voice.

"Then you're the girl everybody's looking for," the trooper said. "A friend of yours rushed into North Newton Headquarters saying you'd been kidnaped."

Kay smiled ruefully. "I'm glad you found me," she said. "But we mustn't waste any time talking about it. I'm afraid the girl I was trying to imitate is in a serious predicament. If that man who captured me thought I was Helene Caldwell, she's in great danger!"

The officer became grave. He helped Kay into the

front seat, saying he would drive the car back to the road where he had left his coupe. But first the officer beamed his light on the license plate.

"Just as I thought," he remarked, "a stolen car. That man never would have dared leave his own."

"I suppose he'll make it hard for the police or anyone else to find him," Kay conjectured.

"But he slipped up on one very important thing," the trooper said. "You had a good look at him and can certainly identify him easily."

"Maybe I can do even better than that," Kay said excitedly. "Have you a pad and pencil?"

The officer looked surprised, but brought them out of his pocket. Quickly Kay began to sketch a man's head as the trooper looked on fascinated. When Kay finished, she smiled in satisfaction.

"Even if I do say so myself, this is a good likeness of my kidnaper. Maybe you can use it to help locate him."

"I'll say we can," the officer replied. "Let's go!"

CHAPTER IX

A JEALOUS BOY

As soon as Kay and Trooper Grayson reached his car, he radioed to North Newton Headquarters to report that the girl had been found and was safe. He also mentioned the stolen car. Suddenly the youthful policeman grinned.

"I'm going to delay your journey home a bit," he said. "About two miles from here is an all-night restaurant. We'll have something to eat."

Kay was grateful. "Wonderful! I'm really famished!"

Kay thoroughly enjoyed the next hour with the policeman. He soon learned of her adventures as a detective and chatted interestingly about things he had learned during his police training.

"You've certainly picked up a baffling mystery," he remarked. "Would you like to tell me about it in more detail?"

Kay was delighted to do so. At the end of her story he complimented her on what she had accomplished so far in tracking down clues.

"That is, with the exception of this last escapade of yours," he said rather severely. "Risking your life is no joke, young lady."

"I suppose I was a bit foolish," admitted Kay wryly.

"But I never dreamed that walking alone in disguise would prove so dangerous."

"At least you have confirmed," the officer said, "that there's much more danger to this whole thing than you anticipated. The person you were with is obviously desperate."

He asked if Kay had any idea what her captor's name was.

"It's only a guess, of course," she replied, "but it might be Tad Bacon. I have a hunch, though, that this isn't his right name and it probably would be hard to trace him by it."

"You're no doubt right," Grayson agreed. "Well, how about some apple pie to top off the meal?"

Kay laughed. "I really couldn't after this feast. Thanks ever so much and now I guess we'd better go."

Half an hour later they reached North Newton police headquarters. Bill Tracey and the Worth twins were standing on the steps. They rushed down to meet Kay and plied her with a hundred questions.

"Let's report to the captain first," Grayson requested.

Kay went inside with the trooper and talked a few minutes with the officer. He congratulated the girl on her escape and advised that in the future she be very careful.

He assured Kay that his men would be alerted to watch for anyone matching her captor's description. She nodded. As Kay walked back outside with Grayson, he gave her a kindly smile and said:

"Maybe you'd better forget the whole mystery. It looks like a pretty dangerous setup to me."

Kay turned startled eyes on him. "Give up?" she asked. "I couldn't let Bro down. He's depending on me so much."

"Well, whatever you do, for Pete's sake, stay clear of people who think you're someone else."

"I'll have a chaperon along next time." Kay chuckled. "And, by the way," she added, "the girl who uses the name Helene Barbara Caldwell—and that may be her real name—is supposed to look a lot like me. If you see or hear any news of her, please let me know."

The group said good-by to the trooper and with Cousin Bill at the wheel started for Brantwood. When they finally reached the little town, the sun was well up and church bells were ringing.

Betty giggled. "We won't get much shut-eye before church," she said, and the other girls drowsily agreed.

Upon reaching home Kay fell into her mother's outstretched arms.

"It's good to see you safe," Mrs. Tracey said, her voice trembling. "What a harrowing experience!"

Bro who wore a look of great relief came forward to shake both of her hands fervently.

"If you had been harmed in any way," he said, his jaw set firmly, "I'd have——"

"Nothing was injured but my pride," Kay said.

Mrs. Tracey insisted that there be no more discussion until later and personally tucked Kay into bed. The girl spent a good part of the day resting and by evening felt refreshed and ready to tackle a little of the school homework which she had been unable to do the day before.

Kay was not able to catch up on her lessons completely and during the following day paid particularly strict attention to her classroom work. It was not until late in the afternoon, after a basketball game between her gym group and another, that she hopefully telephoned the North Newton police headquarters. But the captain had nothing to report on the case.

"Something's bound to break soon," he said cheerfully.

Kay tried to be optimistic also, but she had a feeling the mystery was far from being solved. As for herself, she probably was still in danger.

"Especially if Tad Bacon has found out who I am," she told herself.

As Kay walked along lost in thought a voice said, "Snap out of it!" It was Betty, who continued, "How's your costume for the masquerade coming?"

"Nothing's finished but the red scarf," Kay replied. "I guess I'd better start on it this evening."

After dinner she asked her mother if she would help her work on the gypsy costume. Mrs. Tracey said she would be delighted to and secretly was glad that Kay was not going to pursue her investigation of the mystery immediately.

Cousin Bill was away from home and in order not to leave Bro alone, the two Traceys brought their sewing to the living room. The girl's mother had told her that during the day he had sat for long periods staring into space. They were pleased when he took a sudden interest in the costume making. He asked diffidently if it might be possible to attend the masquerade himself.

"I'd love to have you go," said Kay. "I'll telephone right away about a ticket."

"Oh, would you?" he asked eagerly. "I have a hunch that I may see someone there or that something may happen that will restore my memory."

"Then by all means you're going, even if I have to give up my own ticket." Kay laughed and went to call up the chairman.

When Mrs. Abbott answered, Kay said a friend was visiting and would like very much to have a ticket.

"My goodness, we haven't had any tickets for sale for ages," the woman said and Kay's heart sank.

"I have a very special reason for wanting this person to go," Kay pleaded. "Couldn't you sell just one extra?"

"You mean, Kay, you're working on some mystery," Mrs. Abbott chuckled. "I knew it!"

The girl admitted that this was true and the chairman said she would mail a ticket to the Tracey home. Kay thanked her and went to tell Bro the good news. Suddenly his eyes lighted up.

"I just remembered something," he said. "When my sister and I were little children, Helene was always getting me to dress up and play theater with her. She loved costumes. Do you suppose—do you suppose that she might be going to this masquerade?"

Though Kay saw only an outside chance of this, Bro's suggestion gave her an idea, which she decided to put into action at once. Excusing herself, Kay dashed up the stairs and wrote a note to which she attached a dollar bill and addressed it to North Newton's newspaper, *The Gazette*. It was an advertisement reading:

Wanted: A girl's gypsy costume with a scarf.
Red preferred. Address Box ——.

"This may lead me to Bro's sister!" Kay thought excitedly.

She put a special delivery stamp on the letter. Then after telling the others what she had done, she ran up the street to the mailbox. When she got back to the house, Kay found her mother and Bro engrossed in a conversation about what kind of a costume he might wear to the masquerade.

"Why don't I go as a gypsy boy if you're to be a gypsy girl?" he asked Kay.

"Perfect!" Dropping their work, Kay and her mother took him to the attic, where a trunk full of old clothes was hidden under the eaves. From among the silks and satins in it, Kay selected an old-fashioned red silk blouse with long puffy sleeves for a shirt.

"I can turn this black satin skirt into a pair of breeches in a jiffy," Mrs. Tracey said gaily. "We'll leave a ragged edge to come just below your knees, Bro."

Kay herself donated a large bright yellow scarf. She wound it about Bro's head and tied it in a loose knot at the back.

Her mother had already gone to the second floor to make the trousers and in twenty minutes they were basted together ready to be tried on.

"Dress in the whole costume and come downstairs," she said.

When he appeared Kay declared the outfit was perfect.

"With a mask, no one would ever recognize you," she said, "and you might get one of the prizes."

At this moment the doorbell rang and Kay went to answer it. As she opened the door a cheerful-looking youth with a ruddy complexion smiled at her.

Ronald Earle, who was taking Kay to the masquerade, escorted her to nearly all the high school parties.

"Come in, Ronnie," Kay said warmly.

"Thanks," he replied and stepped inside.

He followed Kay into the living room. Mrs. Tracey greeted him, then Kay introduced Bro. She had told Ronald the situation about the youth and his partial amnesia, but Ronald had not yet met him. He surveyed the boy's gypsy costume in amazement.

Kay laughed. "Oh, Bro has decided to go to the masquerade with us," she explained. "Isn't that wonderful?"

Ronald lost his smile. A look came over his face showing quite plainly he did not think it was wonderful at all. He would much prefer dating Kay alone.

The look was not lost on Bro, for a sad expression filled his eyes. Glancing down at the floor he said:

"Kay, I've changed my mind about going to the masquerade!"

CHAPTER X

GONE!

AT ONCE Ronald realized why Bro had said he would not go to the masquerade. The youth regretted having shown his feelings so plainly, though he would have preferred taking Kay alone.

"Of course you're going," Ronald said, slapping Bro on the shoulder. "It'll be a humdinger of a party."

When the sensitive boy did not reply, Kay told him she would be disappointed if he did not accompany them. Mrs. Tracey also urged him to attend.

At last Bro smiled. "Well, I'll think it over," he said. "In some ways it might be a good idea to go, but in others, well—perhaps I shouldn't show up. After all, I do have an enemy and until my memory is fully restored maybe I'd just better stay close to your home."

Bro said good night and went upstairs, and Mrs. Tracey followed him shortly.

"Kay, I'm terribly sorry about the way I acted," Ronald apologized when they were alone. "I hope I didn't do any real damage."

Kay was sure he had not, but she could not help feeling a little pleased at Ronald's jealousy.

"No harm done, Ronnie," she said, smiling. "But I have an idea."

"What is it?"

"Maybe if you talk to Bro about camp and baseball and football and things you fellows like to do, you can awaken some memory of his past life."

Ronnie was only too glad to try making amends for his seeming unfriendliness. Taking the steps two at a time, he reached the guest room.

"You and I ought to get better acquainted," he said jovially. "How would you like to come over to school some afternoon and watch baseball practice? Not tomorrow but possibly in a couple of days."

"Thanks. Maybe I'll do that," the visitor replied, but without enthusiasm.

There was an awkward pause, then Ronald asked him if he had ever been to summer camp.

"Oh sure," Bro replied, "I used to sail a lot."

Ronald was thrilled by this discovery. "What camp did you go to?" he asked quickly.

Suddenly a blank expression came over Bro's face. He grew somewhat red and admitted that he had no idea.

Ronald, embarrassed again, said, "Forget it, old man!" and changed the subject to football. "Carmont High had a terrific schedule last year, but we did pretty well," he said. "How about your school?"

"Why, it——" Bro stopped and looked at the caller despairingly. Then he asked, "Do you play on the team, Ronnie?"

"Yes. I play center."

Ronald, having run out of school sports topics, turned the conversation to Kay, who, he said, was certainly a wonderful girl. It was amazing how many mysteries she had solved and how many people she had helped.

Bro's response was instant and enthusiastic.

"She and her folks have certainly been swell to me," he said. "Sometimes I think I shouldn't impose on them any longer, but do you know what? Don't ever tell them, but I—I'm afraid to leave here."

"Then by all means you should stay," Ronnie told him. "But why are you afraid?"

"It's a feeling that I've run away from somebody wicked," Bro answered. "I don't know who it is but in my mind he's a scheming old man."

"That would explain why you were slugged in your jalopy," Ronald guessed. "Well, until your memory is completely restored, you couldn't be in a better place than this. Mrs. Tracey is just about the best cook in Brantwood."

Bro laughed. "You're right. My mother was a wonderful cook too."

Ronnie waited expectantly for the youth to say more. Perhaps at last the cloud over his mind was breaking!

But the football center was doomed to disappointment. Although Bro was apparently trying to remember more about the subject he had started, nothing further would come. Heaving a weary sigh, he said:

"Well, I guess I'll go to bed. See you Thursday at the ball field."

Since there was nothing more Ronnie could do, he said good night and went downstairs. Though he reported failure to arouse any helpful memories in Bro, Kay was glad to hear that he had promised to watch baseball practice.

"Oh Mother," she called, seeing Mrs. Tracey come down the stairs.

Kay told her what Ronnie had accomplished and asked if Mrs. Tracey could possibly go with Bro to Carmont when he was ready.

"I have a feeling it wouldn't be safe for him to go by himself," the girl said.

"You're probably right," her mother agreed. "I'll be very glad to accompany Bro. What time does practice begin, Ronnie?"

"Three o'clock."

"Then we'll catch the 2:30 train from here," Mrs. Tracey said.

Ronald talked with Kay a little while about the masquerade, then left.

Wednesday afternoon Kay came home from classes as soon as they were over. Her mother was going to the church bazaar and did not want to leave Bro alone. While putting on her hat, she said to her daughter out of earshot of Bro:

"Dr. Rolfe was here today and I had a long talk with him. He says our visitor is in fine physical condition, but as to his memory, there's no telling how long he may be a victim of amnesia."

"Oh, that's a shame!" Kay exclaimed. "Dr. Rolfe doesn't hold out any hope?"

"He said it was possible that a sudden shock would restore his complete memory. But as to the length of time—who can say?"

"But if we solve the mystery, that will probably do it," Kay said. "I must work even harder on it."

She went at once to the telephone and called *The Gazette* at North Newton. Upon learning there were several replies to her advertisement, Kay excitedly asked the girl in charge to read them to her.

To Kay's disappointment none was from Helene Caldwell.

"Oh dear," Kay thought, discouraged. "All my clues seem to have petered out."

As Kay sat quietly thinking, a more lively scene was taking place in another house. Betty Worth had just arrived home, a large suitbox under one arm.

"Ethel Eaton's costume!" the blond twin said triumphantly to her sister.

"Ethel's costume! What are you doing with it?" Wilma asked.

"Delivering it—after a while. To be exact, the day of the masquerade."

"How'd you get it?"

"Well, I found it," Betty said mischievously. "The dry cleaner left it on the Eaton porch." Betty giggled. "I was afraid it might be stolen so I brought it along."

"And why are you going to keep it?" Wilma demanded.

"Because, dear sister, I found out definitely Ethel Eaton started that horrible gossip about Kay and drew that picture in the lab. And is she going to get away with it? Not if I can help it."

"I can see you're going to play some joke," Wilma said. "What is it?"

Betty chuckled. "Sew this costume up so tight, it will take Ethel one hour to rip the stitches out of it!"

"And be late for the masquerade," Wilma grinned. "That won't bother me."

"Not a word of this to Kay," Betty warned. "She's so softhearted she'd certainly stop me."

"I promise. I wonder how Kay's making out on her costume."

"She said she was going to work on it today."

Kay was very busy on it at this very moment—in fact, her fingers were beginning to ache from the task. Her mother had finished the blouse and Kay was busy on the skirt. She had shirred and sewed on yards and yards of blue and red ruffles, using as a foundation an old tan skirt she had outgrown. In all there were to be ten ruffles. Because Kay was sewing them on so carefully, only four were finished.

"You surely are patient, Kay," said Bro, who had been talking to her as she worked. "Is it necessary to make such fine stitches? It's only a costume."

"I guess I am too fussy," Kay agreed. "Here goes! I'll baste on the rest."

She continued her work but with stitches which grew larger and larger.

"I should just about get through this job before I'll have to prepare dinner. Mother's having supper at the bazaar. Bro, I hope you won't mind a simple meal," she said.

"Not at all," he replied. "But, will your cousin Bill like that?" he asked. "I'll help you. Suppose I bake an apple pie."

Kay looked at the youth in amazement. "You know how to make an apple pie?" she laughed.

"Why sure. I've made lots of them," he said.

"Where?" she asked quickly.

"At camp. I did it to help pay my way——"

Kay waited for him to reveal more but he merely said, "Funny I can't recall where it was."

"You will some time. As to the pie, Cousin Bill and I would love one."

She told him to go ahead, saying she had two more ruffles to sew on, then she would join him.

The work took Kay longer than she had expected. It was close to three-quarters of an hour before she finally finished.

"I'd better slip this costume on to be sure it looks all

right," she told herself. "If not, maybe Mother will fix it."

Carrying the dress to her room, she slipped off her sweater and skirt and tried it on. As she looked into the long mirror on her closet door, Kay was pleased. The costume really was lovely and looked exactly like the one on the magazine cover.

Taking the stencilled red scarf from a bureau drawer, Kay tied it over her head. Then she adjusted the half mask.

"I'm sure no one except my close friends will know who I am," she thought happily.

As Kay took off the costume and put her sweater and skirt back on, her mind turned to Bro's sister. How wonderful it would be if the girl would show up at the masquerade in the gypsy costume and she and Bro could be reunited!

"I wonder how our new cook is making out," she murmured to herself, starting down the stairs.

Upon reaching the kitchen, Kay was amazed not to see Bro. On the table stood a can of flour, some lard, and the box of salt. A pan of apples with a knife beside them lay on the sink. The back door was wide open.

"Bro, where are you?" she called.

When there was no answer, Kay hurried to the back porch and looked around. Their visitor was not in sight.

"Bro! Bro!" she called, panicky, but he still did not respond.

At this moment Bill Tracey drove into the driveway and she flew down to tell him.

"Now Kay, maybe he's only taking a walk, perhaps to the store," he said practically.

But as the minutes passed, it became evident that this was not the case.

"I'm afraid he's run away," the lawyer conceded. "Pretty ungrateful, I'd say."

"Oh Cousin Bill, Bro would never do that!" Kay cried. "Something has happened to him!"

CHAPTER XI

THE SHIP'S CLOCK

"CALL IT a hunch," Kay said to Cousin Bill, "but I have a strong feeling that Bro is in trouble."

"Not necessarily," the lawyer argued. "His memory might suddenly have come back to him."

"But why should that make him run away?"

Bill Tracey reminded his cousin that the youth had been waylaid in his car and robbed of certain papers.

"You know, Kay, this could mean he might have stolen them from someone who slugged him to get them back. If Bro's memory suddenly snapped back—which is usually the way it happens—and he realized that he is a thief, naturally he'd leave here as fast as he could."

"I don't believe anything of the sort," Kay insisted. "I'm going to ask the police to start a search for him."

Cousin Bill shrugged at his cousin's persistence. "Suit yourself," he said, "but after you call them, will you please fix some dinner? I'm starved."

"I promise you a very tasty meal," Kay said, smiling. "You'll be glad you waited!"

A Captain McCarthy happened to be on duty at police headquarters when Kay phoned. After hearing her story and a description of Bro, the officer promised to notify the patrol cars and ask the men to keep their eyes open for the youth. He said there was little they could do, other than that, without any clues.

"I'll try to find you at least one," Kay said and hung up.

She sat deep in thought for several minutes, wondering where she might turn up a clue. Suddenly an inspiration came to her. Picking up the receiver, Kay telephoned Vicki Raponi.

"Hello Kay! This is a coincidence," Vicki said. "I was just about to phone you. But first, tell me why you called."

Kay told the art student of Bro's sudden departure. Vicki was amazed.

"What I have to tell you, Kay, may fit in with Bro's disappearance," she said.

It seemed that, unbeknown to the Raponi family, Helene Caldwell had quietly come to their home that afternoon and taken away her clothes.

"Helene left a note apologizing for not seeing us and saying that she hoped we would understand," Vicki explained.

"And you think," said Kay excitedly, "that she may have come to our house for Bro?"

"It seems reasonable, doesn't it?" Vicki replied.

Kay had to admit that it did. No doubt Tad Bacon had discovered Kay's identity, had found out where Bro was and told Helene.

"If this is the case, have you any idea where they might have gone?" Kay asked.

"No, I haven't," Vicki replied. "But if I should hear anything from Helene, I'll try my best to find out where they are."

"Yes, please do," Kay begged her, and said good-by.

After she had related the phone conversation to Cousin Bill, he said he hoped Vicki Raponi was right in her deduction.

"Now try to forget the mystery for a while, Kay," Bill advised. "I want a good dinner without sugar in my soup and salt in the whipped cream."

"*Whipped cream!* You'll get none of that the way you're bursting out of your clothes these days," Kay replied.

But Kay could not put the mystery out of her mind. She prepared the meal automatically, but every time she saw the flour, sugar and apples which Bro had left so abruptly, she grew more desirous than ever of finding out where he was.

In a short while she and her cousin sat down at the dining room table. Bill Tracey began to talk about news of the day and also praised Kay's cooking highly.

"Your mother couldn't have made better cream of tomato soup," he said, smiling and as she brought on a juicy steak, remarked, "Wow! I couldn't have done better myself."

Kay was not fooled by his joviality. She knew he was trying his utmost to help her forget what seemed like a very ungrateful move on the part of the visitor to whom they had been so kind. As Kay served a fruit dessert, the telephone rang. She fairly flew to the instrument.

"Hello!" came a woman's deep voice. "Is this the Tracey home?"

"Yes."

"I wish to speak to Miss Kay Tracey," the woman went on.

"This is Kay."

In the background of the place from which the woman was phoning, Kay could hear a ship's clock start to strike.

The speaker waited until it had struck six bells, then she said:

"I wish to warn you. Do not hunt for your missing visitor. It will be futile, because you will never see him again!"

The speaker hung up abruptly. Kay replaced the instrument more slowly, stunned by the words she had just heard. Could the woman have been Helene Caldwell disguising her voice? Or did the unknown caller belong to the group who had taken the youth away?

Kay returned to the table and gravely told the lawyer about the warning. But just as the girl completed her recital, she broke into sudden laughter. Bill Tracey looked at her puzzled.

"Now what's the matter?" he asked.

Kay continued to laugh so hard that for several seconds she could not explain the reason for her amusement. Then, finally stifling her chuckles,

"While the woman was talking, I heard a ship's clock striking in the background. I don't think many people happen to have ships' clocks near their telephones. But I know one family that does—Ethel Eaton's!"

Cousin Bill began to laugh too. He praised his cousin for her astuteness and was not surprised when she announced that if Bill did not mind, she would skip dessert and go over to Ethel's house at once.

"Even though Ethel was playing a joke on me, from what she said I believe she knows something about the mystery and I'm going to find out what it is!"

When Kay rang Ethel answered the doorbell. A look of utter astonishment came over her face but she recovered her wits quickly.

"Hello, Kay," she said without enthusiasm. "And what brings you here?"

Kay smiled. "Aren't you going to invite me in, Ethel?" she asked.

The other girl reluctantly did so, but did not go beyond the hall. Again she asked what her caller wanted.

"I came to see your ship's clock," Kay said, her eyes dancing mischievously.

"What for?" Ethel demanded.

"You might call it a study I'm making," Kay replied casually. "May I see it?"

Grudgingly Ethel led the way to a small room which Ethel's father used for an office. Kay looked first at the clock and then at the desk on which the telephone stood.

"Let's see," Kay mused softly. "It's only about ten feet between the clock and the telephone. No wonder I could hear the clock so plainly when it struck six bells."

Ethel's jaw dropped. She knew she was caught squarely, but had no intention of admitting it.

"Ethel, what do you know about Bro?" Kay asked her, looking the girl straight in the eye.

Her schoolmate fidgeted nervously. She would not meet Kay's steady glance and kept tapping one foot on the rug. Finally, in a sullen voice, she replied:

"Why are you so interested in him? What's he to you? I thought he wasn't your real brother."

"You know he isn't," Kay said. "You also realize that I've been trying to help him find out who he is. Have a heart, Ethel, will you? After all, he is an amnesia victim and I'm afraid the poor boy is in trouble. If you know otherwise, tell me."

There was silence in the room for a quarter of a minute before Ethel's defiance weakened. Then she said:

"Oh, all right. After school today I was standing out front waiting for Harry Blackstone. A very handsome man was walking up and down the sidewalk. The minute he spied me, he came rushing over."

Kay suppressed a smile. Ethel could not resist telling the story to revolve around her.

"Of course, he tried to date me," Ethel went on, smirking, "but I couldn't at the time. Then he began to talk about different people in school. After awhile he said he was looking for a girl who called herself a detective."

Ethel paused to give Kay a withering look. Then she continued, "I thought he probably meant you, so what could I do but tell him all about you and Bro," Ethel finished with a shrug.

"You didn't!" Kay cried, sure now her worst fears were justified.

"Well, why shouldn't I have?" Ethel said pointedly. "*I* had—nothing to hide—like some people."

Kay felt like shaking Ethel for the damage she might have caused, but she kept her temper, knowing that she would find out more by letting the unpleasant girl brag.

"Please go on," Kay requested calmly.

"Just before supper, I walked down the street to mail a letter," Ethel explained. "I have a bid to the Spring prom at Radner College."

Kay doubted this, but she responded, "How exciting! I hope you're going."

"I'm thinking it over," Ethel replied haughtily. "Well —about the handsome man. Right after I had mailed my letter, I saw him going toward your house. Naturally, I followed."

Again Kay stifled a giggle. Naturally Ethel would.

"He went around to the back door," the girl continued. "He didn't stay long, though. In about two minutes he came walking out with a boy. I suppose that was Bro."

"Did you speak to them? Or did you hear what they said?" Kay asked excitedly.

Ethel took her time to reply. She knew Kay was eager for what she was about to say and planned to phrase her words carefully to get the fullest effect.

"Well, knowing what I do," Ethel replied, "of course I didn't intrude. I wouldn't want to get mixed up in any affair with that boy."

Again Kay felt a surge of fury at the girl's insinuating manner, but she merely asked if Ethel had any idea where Bro and the stranger were going.

"Yes, to Chicago," she said triumphantly. "I—er—overheard them say so. That's the reason I telephoned you. I thought I'd save you the trouble of further sleuthing."

"Thank you very much for your kindness," Kay said icily.

Personally, she did not believe that Bro and the stranger were headed for Chicago at all. But Kay was convinced that Ethel had really told all that she did know. How much was fact remained to be seen.

"Anything further?" inquired Ethel, obviously enjoying her role.

"Thanks, no," Kay said with dignity and let herself out the front door.

She could sense Ethel's puzzled eyes following her, and knew that the girl was wondering how much Kay believed of her story. Upon reaching home, she found Cousin Bill washing the dishes.

"Oh you lamb!" she cried.

"It's all right—once in a while," he grinned. "What did you find out from your—er—friend Ethel?"

To the lawyer's amazement Kay really had something to report. A frown creased his forehead.

"I'm afraid I was wrong in thinking Bro dishonest," he admitted. "That boy no doubt is in trouble. Have you any idea who Ethel's handsome man might be?"

Kay said she had a very good idea indeed. She was positive it was the man who was using the name Tad Bacon. If he were the ugliest person on earth, Ethel would still have called him handsome.

Mrs. Tracey arrived a little while later and became very upset when she heard what had happened. She had become very fond of their youthful visitor and was extremely concerned about his safety.

"Without his memory it's a double handicap for him," she said. "Oh, if only I could think of some plan of action!"

The evening was not a cheerful one for the Tracey family. Finally they decided to retire. Just as Kay reached her room, the telephone rang. She darted to her mother's room to answer it.

"Kay?" said a faraway voice. "This is Bro! Help me!"

CHAPTER XII

A SEARCH

"Bro! Where are you? Bro!" Kay cried.

She was torn between joyousness at hearing his voice and worry for his safety.

"Old—Stone—Mill——" The boy's voice trailed off.

"What road?" Kay urged.

There was no answer. A hum on the line told her that the connection had been broken.

"Oh dear!" Kay thought desperately. "If this weren't a dial phone, perhaps I could've traced the call."

Even so, the youth's words burned into her brain. *Old Stone Mill!*

"Mother! Cousin Bill!" she called excitedly. "I know where Bro is! He needs our help. We must rescue him right away!"

The lawyer rushed from his room and Mrs. Tracey hurried up the stairway. They listened eagerly as Kay related what she had just heard.

"We'd better hurry," the girl urged. "I'm sure some enemy cut Bro off!"

"The Old Stone Mill shouldn't be too hard to find," the lawyer stated. He picked up the telephone and dialed police headquarters. "McCarthy?" he said. "Is there an old stone mill around here?"

"The only one I ever heard of was torn down a long time ago," the police captain answered.

Bill Tracey repeated the mysterious message that had come to Kay.

"I don't see how anyone could phone from that deserted spot," the officer said, "but I'll order one of the patrol cars to search the area at once."

Half an hour later the captain called back to say that there was no one at the spot where the old mill had stood.

"Are you sure Old—Stone—Mill were the young fellow's words?" McCarthy asked Bill Tracey.

"Suppose you talk to Kay," the lawyer offered.

The girl confirmed the words and asked if there were any farmhouses in the vicinity where there might be an old mill not built of stone.

"I can't think of any offhand," McCarthy replied, "but we'll keep after this thing and let you know."

Another half-hour went by, then he telephoned again. His men had found two farms with old mills and had investigated them. But there had been no sign of the missing youth at either place.

"It's just possible the phone call was a hoax," McCarthy suggested to Kay. "You'd better go to bed, Miss Tracey. No use losing sleep over the case. We'll continue to work all night and if there's anything to the clue, we'll track it down and contact you in the morning."

Kay thanked him, said good-by, then turned to the others.

"I know I shan't sleep a wink," she said. "The phone call wasn't a hoax. Cousin Bill, how about you and I starting out on a search of our own?"

But Mrs. Tracey would not hear of this, saying Kay must let the police take care of it.

"Besides, dear," she added, "what could you accomplish at this hour, and in the dark?"

Kay sighed. Cousin Bill, sensing her disappointment, said, "I'll make a bargain with you, Kay. If the police haven't found out anything by morning, I'll give up business for the day and go searching with you."

"Oh Cousin Bill, you're a darling!" Kay cried. "We'll leave right after breakfast."

"That is, if your mother will let you skip school," the lawyer amended.

Kay turned pleading eyes on Mrs. Tracey. The woman smiled and put an arm around her daughter.

"I know how much this means to you, dear, as well as to Bill and me and Bro. If it's a choice between missing school and rescuing that poor boy, I'll certainly give permission for you to stay away from classes."

Kay hugged her mother and said good night. In her excited state it was hard to go to sleep, but finally she dozed off. At seven o'clock she awoke with a completely new idea on the subject.

"The word *stone* in the old stone mill might be the name of the people who are holding Bro," she thought excitedly.

After showering and dressing quickly, Kay hurried downstairs to tell her mother and Cousin Bill. They were already seated at the breakfast table. Kay kissed them both and sat down herself, plainly showing that she was bursting with an inspiration.

"Well, I can see you have solved the problem of why there are telephones in abandoned mills," the lawyer teased her. "I guess we'll need to know. Police headquarters phoned and said the men have had no luck so far in finding Bro."

"It's a shame!" Mrs. Tracey declared. "But," she added comfortingly, "I'm sure today will bring more hopeful results."

"Thanks for the encouragement, Mother," Kay smiled.

As she ate her oatmeal, Kay told the others what she had figured out.

"Cousin Bill, we can start our hunt by looking for a family named Stone who have an old mill of some sort."

"Very clever," Bill Tracey praised her. "While you eat your breakfast, I'll look up all the Stones in the phone book."

He brought the directory to the table and began jotting them down. After copying the first names of the Stones listed, and their addresses, he looked up.

"Adds up to quite a few. Maybe I'd better start our work by telephoning these folks."

"Oh, don't do that!" Kay objected. "We ought to surprise them. Then when we come to the place where Bro is being held, the people won't have a chance to get away or deny his being there."

"You're right again, little sleuth." Cousin Bill laughed. "I just can't wait for the day when you will come to my office and help me solve those knotty legal problems I get tied up on."

"The tighter the knots, the harder you get tied up?" Kay needled him. "I can just see the new sign on our office door:

*Tracey & Tracey
Legal Binders.*"

The others laughed, then seriously discussed the case as Kay finished her breakfast. When she carried the dishes to the kitchen, her mother insisted upon tidying up alone.

"You go ahead with your search," she said. "The quicker you bring Bro back here, the better I'll feel."

"Yes, let's get started," Bill Tracey urged. "We have a whale of a job ahead of us."

By eight-thirty the cousins were on their way. After three-quarters of an hour they had proved that all the families named Stone in or near Brantwood were respectable people who knew nothing about the kidnaped youth.

"I'm glad we live in a law-abiding community, anyway," Bill Tracey remarked with a grin.

"I am too," Kay said, "but this fact doesn't solve our mystery."

Kay and Bill next tackled the surrounding towns. By lunch time they were weary and discouraged, not having unearthed a single trace of Bro. They went into a restaurant and sat down.

"I'll phone and see if the police have made out any better than we have," Bill suggested. "Please order a roast beef sandwich for me while I call up."

He left the table but came back a few minutes later to say that neither the Brantwood police nor the state troopers had had any success.

"Our own chances of success have narrowed to three farmhouses whose occupants are named Stone," Cousin Bill reminded Kay.

"Not our last chance," the girl disagreed. "It's possible that there's a family named Stone without a telephone."

"You've proved me wrong again," the lawyer conceded, smiling. "If this keeps up——" He made a wry face.

As soon as they finished their lunch, the two set off again on their search. The car speedometer showed they had already traveled more than a hundred miles that morning. Twenty more were added by their calls at the three farmhouses. "And we haven't seen anything yet." Kay sighed.

"Shall we give up and go home?" Bill Tracey asked her, although he knew what the answer would be.

"Of course not," the girl replied firmly. "The next thing we do is look at mailboxes belonging to somebody named Stone who has no telephone." As she saw her cousin's look of dismay Kay added quickly, "Oh, not many farms are without telephones these days. It won't be hard."

"I give in," he said. "I told you I'd take the day off for sleuthing—and I'll keep my promise."

Up one road and down another they went for miles and miles. Not one farmhouse except those previously visited had a mailbox marked Stone.

"Oh where *is* Bro?" Kay worried. "All this time he may be lying helpless in some damp, cold place. After what happened to me, I wouldn't put anything past that heartless Tad Bacon!"

Bill Tracey could not deny this latter statement, but tried to take a more cheerful view of the boy's predicament.

"Even though he's a prisoner, his captor may not be mistreating him," he said.

After they had driven around another hour, the lawyer concluded that Bro must be a long distance from Brantwood.

"Now do we go home?" Bill Tracey asked hopefully.

"I suppose we might as well," Kay replied. She was bitterly disappointed. "But don't go fast," the girl requested. "If we should see a place without a mailbox, I want to investigate it."

The entire farming community, however, seemed to have neat-looking boxes with names prominently displayed. It was not until Kay and her cousin found themselves on a back road some five miles west of Brantwood that Kay suddenly cried out:

"Stop!"

The lawyer had just driven past a battered mailbox Kay had not noticed when they had gone by the place before. The box was attached to a post lying at the side of a lane. Bill Tracey put on the brake and they looked up the narrow lane to a farmhouse which was barely visible from the main road.

"Ramshackle old place," the lawyer remarked. "I guess nobody lives there. And there's no name on the box."

"But look!" Kay called out excitedly. "A telephone wire runs into it. If the place is tumble-down and no one lives in the house, why should there be a telephone?"

"That's right," Bill Tracey agreed. "I'll drive in."

Kay laid her hand on his arm. "I have one of my hunches, Cousin Bill," she said tensely. "What better place to hold a prisoner than a deserted house? And, if Bro is there, we ought to approach quietly; not announce our coming."

Bill Tracey scanned the area. Seeing a clump of trees a short distance down the road, he drove to it and pulled the car in out of sight.

"We'll walk from here," he said. "There are enough trees and bushes along the lane so that we needn't be seen by anyone at the house."

The couple chose opposite sides of the road and carefully picked their way along. Presently they came to a stream and on it was a tumble-down mill.

"Oh, Cousin Bill, this must be the place!" Kay cried excitedly, starting to run.

They neither saw nor heard anything until they were about a hundred feet from the house. Then without warning a large, vicious-looking dog bounded from around the corner of the house straight at them!

At first he growled, then began to bark menacingly. Kay and Bill Tracey dashed behind a thicket. The animal crashed through toward them.

"You'd better run," Bill advised his cousin. "I'll keep him here."

But Kay did not move. Her sudden fright left as she recognized the animal as a breed of bulldog which is not ferocious. Standing her ground, she called:

"Hello, old fellow! Where did you come from? Here boy! Let me pat you!"

Bill Tracey stared at the girl in bewilderment. Then he too realized that the dog would not harm them unless they antagonized him.

The large tawny animal wagged his tail slightly and came toward them diffidently. Kay held out a hand and finally the dog licked it.

"Phew! I thought we were in for a bad time," said Cousin Bill, heaving a sigh. "Well, if his master's at home, he knows by now that company's here."

He and Kay waited, still out of sight, and watched the front door carefully. No one appeared.

"Maybe the dog doesn't belong here," Kay suggested. "I think the coast is clear, Cousin Bill. Come on!"

"All right, we'll take a look."

The two stepped from hiding. The dog followed them, wagging his tail now in friendly fashion. A peek into the windows of the old house proved that the first floor at least was vacant. Kay walked up the front steps and studied the door. Then her eyes wandered to the old-fashioned glass panel above it. Etched on the glass in script letters was one word:

STONE.

"This is it! This is the place!" Kay exclaimed exultantly.

CHAPTER XIII

A SPOOKY PRISON

Cautiously Bill Tracey tried the front door of the deserted house but found it locked. He and Kay walked around to the rear and tested the back door. It, too, would not budge.

"Well," said Kay, "I guess if we're going to investigate, we'll have to break in."

"And that, Miss Tracey," the lawyer replied, "is against the law!"

"Look!" his cousin cried, pointing to a second floor window. "It's boarded up! That might be Bro's prison."

Bill Tracey agreed. Cupping his hands around his mouth, he called loudly:

"Bro! Bro! Are you here?"

Bill and Kay listened intently for an answer. Did they hear one, or were their imaginations playing tricks on them?

"Hello!" Kay cried at the top of her lungs. "Bro, it's Kay!"

Again she and her cousin strained their ears to catch any reply. This time there was no mistake. They plainly heard a voice, even though it was muffled. Bill Tracey had no compunctions now about entering the premises.

"How to get in, though, stymies me," he said.

"Maybe one of the first floor windows isn't locked," Kay suggested.

She offered to try those on two sides of the house, while he investigated the windows on the others. Within half a minute Kay called excitedly:

"I've found one that's unlocked!"

She tried to raise it but was not strong enough. Her cousin came on a run and gave the sash a hard push. The window opened stubbornly, but finally there was a space large enough for them to get through. Bill Tracey boosted Kay up, then climbed in himself. The air within was dank and musty.

Without pausing a second to investigate the first floor rooms, Kay raced up the creaking stairway ahead of him and went directly toward the bedroom from which she surmised the voice had replied. There was a heavy wooden bar across the door, which was locked as well. An iron key remained in the lock.

"Bro! Are you in there?" Kay called loudly.

"Yes! Oh, you're here at last," came the faint answer.

Bill Tracey, close on Kay's heels, lifted the wooden bar out of place, while his cousin turned the key. The door was pulled open from the inside, and Bro faced them.

"You found me!" he half-sobbed, grabbing their hands gratefully. "I was so afraid you hadn't understood what I meant on the telephone."

"It had us stumped at first," the lawyer remarked. "But Kay's super brain figured it out. Are you all right?"

The youth insisted he was none the worse for his adventure and pointed to a basket of food on the floor, saying his kidnaper had left it. Bill Tracey gave a low whistle.

"The fellow was all prepared for the kidnaping, eh?" he commented.

Bro, suddenly looking over their shoulders, gave a cry of terror as he saw the huge dog leaping down the hall. Without ceremony he pulled Kay and her cousin into the bedroom and slammed the door shut.

"He's vicious!" Bro gasped. "We'll never get out of here."

The animal began to whine at the door and then started barking.

"He's not vicious at all," Kay explained, and before Bro could stop her opened the door again.

The dog bounded to Kay who patted and stroked him.

"You mean—you mean that dog——" Bro leaned weakly against the wall.

"What is it?" prompted Kay gently.

The youth recovered somewhat and went on to explain.

"When I found out the man was a double-crosser, I started to fight him. He set that dog on me. He'd had him hidden. The beast looked ferocious so I ran. I landed in this room, and then that guy locked me in."

"What for?" the lawyer asked.

"He didn't tell me."

"Did you find out his name?"

"No."

"He could have been the same one who tied me up," said Kay.

"Oh, I don't think so," Bro replied quickly. "This one wears a mustache and had fat cheeks."

"He could have fixed himself up that way as a disguise," the girl told him. "I believe he was Tad Bacon. Is he the man you left our house with?"

Bro, surprised, nodded and asked her how she had

found this out. Kay merely replied that a girl she knew had seen the two together.

"We want to hear your story from beginning to end," Bill Tracey interrupted. "But I think it advisable if we get out of this house first and find a safe place to sit down."

The group went outdoors, the dog following them dutifully. They seated themselves under a large tree out of sight of the lane from where they could watch for anyone coming.

"I'm terribly ashamed that I left so suddenly," Bro said contritely. "Please forgive me. You Traceys have been so kind. I had no business to go off without telling you."

"You're not to worry about that at all." Kay smiled at him. "Just tell us what happened."

The youth said that he had just collected all the ingredients for the apple pie he planned to make when there was a knock on the back door.

"I opened it and saw a man standing there. He said that if I'd go with him he'd take me to my sister. I was surprised, of course," Bro continued. "But I did have sense enough to demand proof of what he said. He told me my sister had sent a password."

"What was it?" Kay asked eagerly.

"Red Scarf," the youth replied. "After that I didn't have any doubt and asked him where she was. He wouldn't tell me—said this was a secret—and I'd have to go along to see Helene.

"I agreed to do this but when I said I must go upstairs and tell you, Kay, he got kind of nasty. He insisted that if I didn't come at once, my sister wouldn't wait for me."

"Such nonsense!" Bill Tracey burst out.

"I know that now," Bro said ruefully. "But at the time

I guess I was so anxious at the chance to find Helene, I didn't think too clearly. I was planning to phone you, Kay, as soon as I met my sister."

"But you never got the chance until after you were a prisoner?" Kay guessed. "Where is the phone, by the way, and why is there one in this empty house?"

"Search me," Bro answered. "It was in the closet of that room. I'd just called you when I heard that man coming and hid it. I guess he knew about the phone, though, because later it was dead. He probably cut the wire."

"No doubt," Cousin Bill agreed. "Go on."

Bro said that after he and the stranger had walked about two blocks from the Tracey home, he stopped at a car and said they would ride the rest of the way.

"I got in," Bro explained, "and that was the most foolish thing I ever did in my life, I guess. As we drove into this deserted place I began to be suspicious and told him I wanted to get out. With that, he grabbed hold of me and said——"

Bro's usually boyish expression became grim for a moment, as he paused. The Traceys wisely did not ask questions. Finally he continued slowly:

"The man said I'd have to go with him—that I didn't remember who I was but *he* knew and that I'm a thief! My sister Helene would protect me, but the Traceys would turn me over to the police as soon as they found out."

The youth looked beseechingly at his friends. "You—you don't think I'm a thief, do you?" he said almost desperately.

"If I'm any judge of human nature," Bill Tracey answered staunchly, "you're certainly no thief."

"We believe in you and will stick by you," added Kay.

"Thank you both," Bro said simply. "That man said I had stolen some valuable papers. Although I can't remember, I just have a feeling they were stolen from *me!*"

"Did this man ever mention Chicago in his conversations?" Kay asked, recalling Ethel's remark to this effect.

"No, he didn't. He never told me his name, either or where he comes from."

The dog, who had been lying quietly at Kay's feet, now showed signs of restlessness. They all wondered if his master might be coming back and stood up, waiting tensely. But no one came in view.

"Maybe the dog's master isn't very far away," Kay suggested. "Why don't we see if he'll lead us to him?"

"Good idea," Cousin Bill agreed.

Kay ran around a bit, and the dog leaped joyfully behind her and barked. Kay kept up this game for a few minutes, then said:

"Where's your master? Go get your master!"

The dog looked up at her, cocked his massive head and wagged his tail. He evidently wished to continue playing.

"Go home!" Kay cried, clapping her hands. "Go home, old fellow! Find your master!"

This time the dog seemed to understand. As if being scolded, he put his tail between his legs and started off. He took a direction in back of the farmhouse which led across a hill. Bro and the Traceys followed quickly.

"I see a house way over there," Kay said, panting, as they reached the brow of the hill. "That must be where the dog's going."

The house proved to be farther away than they had thought and cousin Bill was puffing by the time they reached it. Two small boys were playing in the yard and the dog ran up to them gleefully.

"Hi, Rover!" one of the boys said. "Where have you been?" Then he noticed the three callers. "Hello!" he chirped.

The other little fellow said hello also and Kay asked where their daddy was.

"He's in the Army," the older boy replied.

"Then I guess he's not here," Kay said.

"No, he's with the soldiers." The boy began to march around imitating one. "Do you want to see my mother?" the boy asked without a pause in his erect walking.

"Yes, please."

"Mother! Moth-er!" both little boys cried together.

A pretty young woman came out of the back door and greeted the trio. "May I help you?" she asked pleasantly.

"We followed your dog here from the Stones' deserted farmhouse across the hill," Kay said. "Do you know who owns it now?"

The woman looked surprised and replied, "You're the second person in the past two days who has asked me that same question. I don't think the place is for sale yet. The members of the Stone family have died but I believe the property is tied up in some kind of court case."

"Would you mind telling us who else was inquiring about the place?" Bill Tracey asked with a casual air.

"A man who said his name was Hamm," the woman replied.

Despite the seriousness of the case, Kay had to smile. She had expected the woman to mention the name Bacon; instead she had said Hamm. The girl wondered whether Bro's enemy called himself by various food names and what the significance might be. Foolish though the idea seemed, she determined to remember it as a clue.

"Did Mr. Hamm borrow your dog?" Kay asked the woman.

"I hadn't thought of it that way," she replied. "He seemed to take a liking to Rover and urged him to go along when he walked across the hill to the old Stone place. I never saw the man again, and Rover came home by himself late last night."

Kay and Bill exchanged glances. Should they tell her what happened? At a slow nod from the lawyer, he and Kay took her out of earshot of the children and disclosed part of the story to her.

"If that man ever comes here again, be sure to call the police," Bill Tracey advised. "And now I'd like to use your phone to call them."

"It's in the kitchen," the woman said. "I'll show you. What a horrible experience for that poor young man!"

When they came outside again, Kay said, "Thank you very much. We must go now. Our car's parked over on the other road."

The group waved good-by to the little boys and returned across the hill. Bill Tracey said the police had promised to station a guard at the old farmhouse at once. They waited until a trooper came, then went down the lane to their own car.

All this time there had been no sign of Bro's kidnaper and during the drive the youth was very glum. He did not speak and gazed out of a side window, a worried frown creasing his forehead.

"I must get him out of this mood," Kay thought, "or he'll be ill. His amnesia might even become worse!"

Suddenly she recalled that Bro had seemed interested in meeting Ronald and watching the high school baseball practice.

"That might cheer him up," she told herself. "If we hurry, there's still time for Bro to see some of it. And I ought to find out about my homework anyhow." Aloud she said, "Cousin Bill, will you please drive us to Carmont instead of Brantwood? I want to stop at school."

The lawyer obligingly took the next turn which led to Carmont, saying he would like to do an errand in town too. At the high school Kay asked Bro to go with her. She took him to the ball field and said she would come back there for him in a little while. As she walked away, the girl was delighted to see from his intense interest in the game that her plan had worked.

Kay walked back to the main building to go in the front door. As she entered, Kay came face to face with Betty and Wilma Worth.

"Well, where in the world have you been?" Betty asked.

"Sleuthing. Tell you about it later."

"You mean—you weren't ill?" Wilma asked, a worried look crossing her face.

"No. Should I have been?" Kay asked, chuckling.

The twins looked at each other wide-eyed. Then Betty said soberly, "I have bad news for you, Kay. Miss Elston sprang a math quiz on us. She announced that anybody who was absent today for any reason except illness would flunk for the month!"

CHAPTER XIV

THREE MUSKETEERS

"I'VE FLUNKED!" Kay cried, staring at Betty as if she could not believe this.

"That's what Miss Elston said—anybody who wasn't ill but didn't take the quiz today would get a big fat goose egg for this month," the twin replied.

Kay announced that she would go to see the math teacher at once. "I believe Miss Elston will relent if I explain——"

"And teacher's pet," broke in a sarcastic voice behind her, "will no doubt have the decision reversed." The speaker was Ethel Eaton who giggled unpleasantly and walked on.

After the unfriendly girl had left the building, Betty said, "Don't go, Kay, until you tell us what happened today."

Although eager to see Miss Elston, Kay gave the twins the whole story. They listened almost spellbound.

"This case is getting dangerous," Wilma said when Kay had finished and added with a faraway look:

> *Tarry not where danger hovers,*
> *Lest it catch thee unaware.*
> *Flee, oh flee the treacherous trap,*
> *Only fools will take a dare.*

"Oh, Wilma, you give me a pain," Betty said, making a wry face at her sister. "There wouldn't be any fun in this life at all if you didn't take a dare once in a while."

"Just the same," said Wilma, "there's no sense sticking your head into a noose."

Kay laughed, saying she would not comment and hurried off. She telephoned her mother that Bro had been found and that they were at the school.

"Oh, I'm so relieved!" Mrs. Tracey said. "And he's all right?"

"Yes. But he had a bad fright."

After a little more conversation, Kay hung up and went on to Miss Elston's room, hoping to catch the teacher before she left.

Fortunately the woman was still at her desk. She smiled at Kay, asking if she had been ill that morning.

"No, Miss Elston," said Kay. "That's why I came to talk to you. When you hear my reason for being absent, I'm sure you'll excuse me."

"What is the reason?"

Quickly Kay gave the woman the highlights of the case on which she was working and ended with her recent sleuthing adventure.

"My goodness!" the teacher exclaimed. "You're very convincing, Kay. I feel as if I had just read a thrilling mystery story." She smiled at the girl. "I'll permit you to take the make-up quiz with the students who were absent because of illness."

"Thank you, Miss Elston."

Kay was about to leave when the teacher asked her to wait a minute. "It's just possible that I might be able to help you solve this case," she said.

"Wonderful!" Kay said. "How, Miss Elston?"

The woman explained that when she started as a

teacher she was not able to get a high school position. She had, therefore, taught for a while in a grade school in Rose City—the fourth grade to be exact.

"In my class was a lovely little girl named Helene," she said. "Even at that age she seemed pretty talented in art. Five years later I had her brother in my class. His name was Dick.

"He was a handsome little fellow, but never very strong. He was not able to take part in strenuous athletics."

"What was Helene and Dick's last name?" Kay asked excitedly.

"That's the trouble," Miss Elston answered. "Ever since I've been talking to you, I've been trying to remember it. I'm provoked at myself that I can't think of it. Somehow I connect the name with food or cooking. But that may be because both children liked to cook."

Kay was gazing out the window, a faraway look in her eyes. She had thought Tad Bacon's real name might be like that of a food. Could he be related to Dick and his sister?

"The name may come to me later," Miss Elston went on. "But anyway, I thought if I could meet this young man you call Bro, I might possibly recognize him."

"We'll do that right away if you can spare the time," Kay said. "Bro is watching the baseball practice."

"How fortunate!" the woman said, and the two set off for the field.

"Bro is the boy standing next to Ronald Earle," Kay told her companion. "Will you do me a favor, Miss Elston? Walk up and down past him without my going along. If you think he's Dick, I'll call him by that name suddenly, imitating Helene's voice. It may help to restore his memory."

The teacher agreed and walked off. Returning to Kay a few minutes later, she said the youth certainly resembled the one who had been in her fourth grade class.

"Then I'll try my stunt," Kay said excitedly.

Together they walked back to where Bro was standing. Quite unexpectedly Kay said to him:

"Dick!"

"Yes, Helene," the youth replied, but without turning. He was intently watching a batter make a homerun.

Kay grabbed Miss Elston's arm elatedly. Then covering her face with one hand, she said:

"Dick, you remember Miss Elston from fourth grade, don't you?"

With this the youth spun around and looked at the teacher. Then he smiled. "Why yes, I remember Miss Elston. How are you?"

"Why I'm fine, Dick. How are you?" the teacher said.

Then, as quickly as the recognition had come, the eagerness faded from Bro's eyes. He looked toward Kay, who for a moment he had once more thought was his sister. The girl, knowing the little scene was over, put her hand down. Smiling at the youth, she said:

"I'm so glad we've learned your name's Dick. What's the rest of it?"

"How I wish I knew!" the boy said. Then, looking at the woman beside Kay, he asked in embarrassment, "What did you say your name is?"

Kay told the story all over again and reintroduced Miss Elston. Dick said he was extremely sorry but he did not recall ever having lived in Rose City or being in Miss Elston's fourth grade.

"Never mind," said Kay kindly. "We have a wonderful clue anyway."

She urged the boy to continue watching the baseball

practice in which he seemed to be keenly interested. As he turned back, Kay and the teacher walked up the road-way.

"Thanks a million," Kay said to the woman. "You've really helped a great deal."

"I hope to help still more," Miss Elston said. "I'll try very hard to think of Dick's last name. In the meantime I'll write to the school principal in Rose City to see if he can help us."

"Oh, if he only can!" Kay cried.

"I'll let you know as soon as I hear anything," Miss Elston promised.

Kay saw Cousin Bill coming in his convertible and hopped in when he pulled up. When she told him of the latest clue he was keenly interested at once.

"If the school isn't able to give us the information, I might track down their name through legal sources in Rose City."

He picked up Bro and Ronnie and drove them all back to Brantwood. That evening after dinner the Traceys tried to help Dick remember his last name by calling off all kinds of food which in any way resembled a proper name.

"Peach, apple, plum," Bill Tracey suggested, but Bro shook his head.

"Bean, pepper, kale," was Mrs. Tracey's contribution.

Dick laughed, saying he did not know whether the words were close or not.

"Maybe it's something like Cook or Baker," Kay offered.

"Nice names, but not mine," Bro replied.

At last they gave up. Kay turned to her homework and at ten o'clock went to bed. She was up early and reached the railroad station in good time without racing. Betty and Wilma also were there and in a few minutes Ethel Eaton joined them.

"Good morning, Kay," Ethel said. "What's the latest news from the Tracey Police Bureau?"

"Everything's okay," Kay replied.

When she said no more, Ethel looked annoyed. "Hmph! After all the help I gave you about that handsome man who wanted to date me, I don't think you need to be so stingy with your information," she flung back.

"Well," said Kay, a teasing look in her eyes, "I'll give you a little hint, Ethel. As you know I skipped school yesterday. I went hunting for a boy I called Bro. And what do you think? I came home with one named Dick."

Betty and Wilma as well as Ethel turned puzzled and questioning eyes on Kay. The twins knew enough not to speak up at this moment—Kay apparently had discovered something since they had seen her the afternoon before. She would tell them at the proper time what it was.

But Ethel, devoured by curiosity, was determined to find out more about what Kay had just told them. She asked several questions before waiting for an answer. Kay merely smiled, saying:

"Really, Ethel, I've told you all I can. And here comes our train. I'll see you at the masquerade tonight."

"Oh of course. And you're going as a gypsy?" Ethel said sweetly, now enjoying her own little joke of letting Kay know she had found out what the other's costume was to be. "I'm going as a grand lady. I shan't tell you exactly what my costume is though." She giggled. "I don't know myself yet."

Kay and the twins exchanged glances. What did Ethel mean?

"Why," Wilma remarked blandly. "I thought your dress was all set."

As the train thundered into the station, Ethel said above the noise, "It was—but what do you know? The cleaner lost the duchess costume I was going to wear. They're sending me another one though, even better."

Betty looked crestfallen. What about her trick!

CHAPTER XV

THE RED DEVIL

As ETHEL flounced up the aisle of the train, Kay and the twins seated themselves near the door. Betty was gloomy indeed over the announcement that the dry cleaner was going to supply Ethel with another costume.

"She put one over on you that time," Wilma teased, and told Kay of her sister's fizzled prank.

"That girl makes me positively ill," Betty stormed. "Here I thought I had it all fixed up so she wouldn't get to the masquerade until late, and now she'll probably be the first one there."

"And make life miserable for you," Wilma remarked.

Kay had an idea. "Maybe the cause isn't lost yet," she chuckled. "Betty, when we get to school, why don't you call up the mother of the boy who was going to deliver the costume, and ask him to take it to the Eaton house this noon? Then Ethel's mother will probably call the establishment and cancel the order for the other costume."

"Bright girl!" Betty said. "I'll do that."

When they reached the Carmont station, Betty ran ahead of the others so that she could put a phone call into Brantwood before classes began. The boy's mother promised that her son would do the errand that noon.

During morning classes Kay found a flutter of excitement among her schoolmates. Many of them planned to attend the masquerade and there was a good deal of buzzing about costumes and dates.

"Why don't you girls come to my house to dress?" Kay invited the twins as she and the Worths were walking into math class. "The boys can pick us up there."

"Okay," Betty agreed.

As the students walked toward their seats, Miss Elston beckoned to Kay. She whispered that she had sent a letter air mail to Rose City and hoped for an early response. Again Kay thanked her and then took her seat.

Before beginning her lecture the teacher returned the quiz papers from the day before. Kay and the twins saw Ethel make a wry face and were sure that she had not received a good mark—at least, not as good as she felt she was entitled to. Her face grew even blacker when Miss Elston announced the names of those who would be permitted to take a make-up quiz and heard Kay Tracey's read among the others.

"It just isn't fair," she mumbled under her breath.

No one paid any attention to Ethel and the morning's work went on. During lunch hour in the cafeteria, Betty saw a student come in and tell Ethel that she was wanted on the telephone. Thinking that the message might be about the costume, Betty followed Ethel and lingered near the telephone booth in the main hall. When the other girl came out a few minutes later, Betty "accidentally" passed her.

"Everything set for tonight, Ethel?" Betty smiled sweetly.

"Yes," Ethel replied with a sigh. "Those dumb cleaners finally found my duchess costume. Now I won't have to wear a substitute." She pulled herself up to her full height. "I can carry the duchess role very well. I expect to win that cruise!"

She swept majestically down the hall as Betty tried to stifle her giggles. A few minutes later she met Kay and Wilma and reported her success.

"Poor Ethel!" Wilma sighed. "Can't you just see her ripping and ripping——"

"And getting ripping mad?" Betty added. "Well, I don't feel one bit sorry for her. The way she treated you, Kay——"

A bell rang and the girls returned to their studies. When classes were over, they hurried back to Brantwood because an early dinner had been planned at both homes. This would leave plenty of time for putting on costumes, make-up, and fixing their hair. When Kay reached the house and swung gaily into the living room, she found their guest reading a book. She thought he looked a bit sad.

"Hello, Dick!" she said. "Any news?"

"No, Kay. I've thought and thought all day what my last name may be, but nothing has come to me."

"Well, don't think any more about it," the girl advised kindly. "Just put your mind on the masquerade and all the fun you'll have."

To her dismay, the youth said he was not going. It took nearly half an hour to convince him he should change his mind.

"Your costume is ready," Kay said, "and you needn't remove your mask at any time if you don't want people to see you. Personally, I think it would be a good idea to leave the mask off. In that big crowd, someone may recognize you and that's just what we want."

"It's not what I want," Dick said. "I've been thinking about that man who kept me a prisoner. He said I was a thief and you know, Kay, he could be right."

Kay looked the youth directly in the eye. "If you're a thief, then I'm the world's worst monster. Come on, snap out of it! You never stole anything in your life. You're going to the masquerade and that's all there is to it."

At last the boy yielded. From that moment on he became cheerful and helped prepare dinner. He and Kay ate together. Mrs. Tracey said she would wait for Bill, who would be late.

About six-thirty the twins arrived with their costumes. The three girls went upstairs and into the shower. There was a good deal of giggling and teasing among them. Betty, who was dressed first, looked really dashing in her green habit.

"Maybe Robin Hood will be at the dance and ask you to go hunting with him," Wilma spoke up.

Betty laughed. "Hunting for girls, you mean? Not me. Even if I'm one of Robin Hood's merry men, I don't want to dance with girls."

"You could do worse," Kay spoke up.

"Wilma," said Betty after a while, "you look simply adorable dressed in that shepherdess costume. Just like a Dresden china doll. If you would stand still and stop breathing, somebody might buy you for a picture window."

"Well, of all things," said Wilma indignantly, ignoring the compliment, "I won't stop breathing for anyone!"

Kay came in for her share of teasing when she put on her gypsy costume. Wilma said she ought to put up a tent in the middle of the dance floor and collect a few pennies reading palms.

"Although I for one," she added, "would hate to have

you tell my fortune. You'd probably involve me in some horrible mystery."

Mrs. Tracey came to the door to say that their escorts were downstairs. As the three girls descended the steps, they gazed in bewilderment. Below them stood the three famous musketeers, dressed exactly alike. With their masks on, they were hardly distinguishable from one another.

"We aim to confuse you girls tonight," said one of the boys whose voice belonged to Jim Becker, who was taking Betty.

"You three look pretty nifty," said another. No mistaking that deep voice. It was Ronnie's.

The third musketeer was Don Wilcox, Wilma's date.

When Dick came downstairs in his gypsy boy's costume he was introduced to Jim and Don and then the young people set off for the dance. Kay and Dick rode with Ronald, who offered to let them off at the main entrance of the Carmont High School before finding a place to park the car.

"Oh, I'd like to walk," said Kay. "We'll go with you."

There was such a jam of cars that it became necessary to park three blocks away from the school. As the three alighted and started walking, Kay suggested that they adjust their masks to avoid recognition.

"I'll have to distinguish you somehow from the other musketeers," Kay said to Ronald. "I guess by the dimple in your chin."

Dick laughed, but Ronald did not. From early childhood, he had hated that dimple in his chin.

"What a crowd of people!" Kay remarked as they climbed the long steps to the front corridor of the school.

The masqueraders were forced to form a line to go past ticket takers. It was nearly ten minutes before Kay and the boys were admitted. As the girl presented her ticket, the man taking them looked at her strangely and remarked:

"What's the idea of coming in twice?"

Kay paused a moment to inquire what he meant, but she was shoved ahead by several people eager to get to the dance.

"Meet you downstairs in the gym," Ronald said to her, as he and Dick went off to check their coats.

The girls' cloakroom was in the opposite direction. As Kay headed for it, she kept thinking about the ticket taker's remark. Was it possible that there was another costume at the masquerade like hers? Could it be Helene who was wearing it?

Again Kay was forced to stand in line. Several minutes elapsed before she could check her coat and make her way down the stairs to the gymnasium. Ronald was not in sight, but Kay was so interested in watching the various masqueraders that she did not mind the wait.

"How lovely that queen looks!" the girl thought, gazing at a tall young woman in a glistening white dress with a crown of rhinestones on her head.

There was a lovely French powder puff ballet dancer, a girl in a skating costume, an Indian with a long feathered headdress, and a picturesque looking old-time stage-coach driver with a sweeping handle-bar mustache.

One couple were dressed as rag dolls with brightly rouged cheeks and dishmop wigs. There was another colorful character costumed as a jack-in-the-box, and Kay marveled at the way he maneuvered himself, the box, and his partner through the tightly-packed roomful of people.

A moment later Kay paused to admire a stalwart young man dressed as a Christmas tree, with a bright star wink-

ing on and off at the top. She guessed that he must have a
battery concealed somewhere on his person and thought
how clever this was.

Suddenly Kay's arm was grasped tightly. She turned
and looked quickly at the person who had grabbed her.
He was dressed in a Red Devil's costume, his face completely covered.

"Let go of me!" Kay ordered. "You're hurting my
arm."

"And I ought to hurt you more," the man said in a
deep voice. "Why did you come here?"

Evidently the devil had mistaken Kay for someone
else!

"Listen, you," the man said, squeezing Kay's arm so
hard she winced with pain, "if you remove your mask
once during the evening, that pretty face of yours will
never look the same! Who's your date?"

As Kay kept silent, the iron grasp on her arm tight-
ened.

CHAPTER XVI

KAY'S DOUBLE

AFTER a struggle Kay managed to pull away from the
Red Devil.

"Don't you get out of my sight!" the man warned.
"Helene, I asked you: Who is your date?"

Kay decided this man must have some power over the
girl he thought she was. Kay would pretend to appear
afraid of him.

"Can't you see I'm alone?" she replied to his question
as to who her escort was.

"Well, you'd better be," the man said roughly. Leaning close to her, he added, "You may stay exactly one-
half hour and then I'm taking you home. You had no
business to come here."

Kay, seeing Ronald on his way toward her and knowing that he would help her out, looked up at the Red
Devil and smiled. She decided to take a chance on learning something.

"Oh, Tad!" she said wistfully.

The devil did not act at all surprised at her remark. He
merely said, "Well, okay, Helene. One hour then. But
don't get out of my sight, you little thief!"

So he *was* Tad Bacon! Kay's ruse had worked! He

took hold of the girl as if he were about to dance off with her when Ronald reached them.

"Say," he said, shoving the devil aside, "what's the idea? This is my dance."

Kay was fearful that Ronnie would give away her secret. She quickly excused herself to Tad and literally pulled her escort away from the devil.

"What's going on here?" Ronnie asked. "And who's that guy?"

Quickly Kay told him what had happened and her suspicions regarding the man.

"He can't get away with this!" the youth declared.

He released his partner, saying he was going right back and punch the fellow. Kay grabbed the boy's arm.

"Oh, Ronnie, please don't!" she begged. "I'm sure I'm on the brink of solving this mystery and everything might be spoiled if Tad gets wind of it."

Ronald paused. Then he put his arm around Kay and they danced off.

"If there's another girl here dressed like you, Kay, you're both heading for trouble," he prophesied. "Why don't we settle this thing right now?"

"That's just the point," said Kay. "We mustn't let the devil find the other girl before we learn who Tad Bacon really is."

"This is a jigsaw puzzle all right," Ronald remarked. "Let me know when I can help."

The couple danced for two minutes in silence. Then Ronald said he had an idea.

"Chuck Winters is coming to the masquerade as a comic cop. What say we turn him into a real policeman?"

Kay laughed. "Ronnie, you're a genius."

In whispered tones the two plotted how they would

capture Tad Bacon. Apparently Chuck had not arrived
yet for he was not among the dancers.

"I hope Chuck didn't change his mind and come in another disguise," Ronald said several minutes later.

The music stopped and the couple walked into the
corridor. But the intermission was short and soon they
were back on the dance floor. In a moment they passed
Betty Worth. The girl whispered:

"The royal duchess isn't here yet!"

Kay chuckled and went on with Ronnie. As they
searched for the comic cop, Kay kept thinking about the
Red Devil's remarks to her. He had accused Helene of
being a thief! Probably he was the same man who had accused her brother Dick of being a thief also. Was the man
blackmailing the girl? And had he been blackmailing
Dick before the boy lost his memory?

This reasoning brought another disturbing thought to
Kay. "Ronnie, I haven't seen Bro since we got here. I
hope nothing has happened to him."

Ronald was a bit concerned himself. Although he had
said little on the subject, he was worried not only for
Kay's safety but that of Helene and her brother Dick as
well. Tad Bacon's costume as a Red Devil no doubt
suited him well!

But Ronnie shook off his fears. "Dick has probably
found some attractive girl and is walking outside with
her," he said.

"I'd like to tell Dick that his sister may be here," Kay
said. "Let's amble around the corridors and see if we can
find him."

When they came to one of the dance floor exits, the
couple walked out. Dick was not in sight, so Kay and
Ronnie climbed to the floor above and strolled around
the corridors there. They finally found the gypsy-clad

boy in a classroom. He was seated at one of the desks reading a book.

"Why, Bro!" Kay cried, rushing in. "You should be down in the gym dancing."

The youth looked up at her sadly. "Everyone seemed to have a partner," he said.

"Oh, you shouldn't give up trying," Kay laughed. "*I* want to dance with you right now."

"Do you really?" Bro cheered up instantly. "That would be swell!"

The youth arose and went with her and Ronald to the floor below. On the way Kay told Dick that she suspected his sister might be there in the same kind of costume Kay was wearing.

"My sister!" Dick cried. "If she only were!"

Kay revealed her little fracas with the Red Devil and her suspicions regarding the man. The girl also told him how she and Ronnie planned to capture the fellow, using the masquerading comic cop and he laughed.

"I'll look for Chuck in the coat room," Ronnie said. "Be seeing you."

He left them and the couple entered the gymnasium. Dick proved to be an excellent dancer and Kay thoroughly enjoyed herself.

"Where did you learn to dance so well?" asked Kay, who was a very good dancer herself, but Dick could not remember.

The couple executed several tricky tango steps and Kay's red and blue gypsy skirt swung in rhythm to the music.

In no time at all two couples near them had stopped dancing to watch Kay and Dick. When the number was finished several people clapped and called out gaily to them:

"Encore!"

Kay caught sight of Ethel Eaton, the duchess, gazing jealously. The part of her face showing below her mask resembled the blackest kind of thundercloud. The orchestra began to play a lilting waltz, and Kay and Dick commenced dancing to the gay music.

All this time Kay had kept her eyes open for any sign of another costume like her own. She did not see one but in a few minutes the Red Devil passed them again.

"Is he the one who thinks you're Helene?" Dick asked Kay.

"Yes."

Uneceremoniously the youth left her, dashing through the crowd after the man. Just as quickly Kay raced after him and grabbed Dick's arm before he could tackle the hooded masquerader. Fortunately the man had his back to them.

"Please, let's dance some more," Kay said.

Dick obeyed but kept looking over his shoulder at the disappearing figure in red. He asked why Kay had stopped him.

"Because I'm afraid it might spoil our plans," she replied. "Ronnie is going to take care of that end of things. Let's you and me keep on hunting for your sister."

The youth agreed and the couple circled the big gymnasium again. It was difficult to try spotting all the dancers, so Kay suggested that they go up to the balcony and look down on them. Upon reaching it, they realized that the floor was almost solid with dancers, who were unable to move except at a snail's pace.

"It would be hard to find Helene even from here," Dick remarked after a few minutes.

"Let's do it systematically," Kay said. "You take the left hand side of the room and I'll take the right."

They stood in silence for nearly five minutes, quickly scanning each person on the floor. At last both had to concede that if any girl were at the party in a gypsy costume like Kay's, she was not among the throng below.

An alarming thought came to Kay at this point. Suppose Helene had been so afraid of the Red Devil that she had left the party as soon as she spotted him! On the other hand, she argued, Tad had seemed surprised to find the gypsy there, so it was possible Helene did not know what costume Tad was wearing. Kay said to Dick:

"Maybe the ticket taker was wrong."

"You mean my sister may not be here?" Dick looked disappointed.

"Yes. With all this crowd, I don't see how that man could possibly remember costumes so exactly. Look down toward the center of the floor. There's a girl with a gypsy costume but it's nothing like mine."

Dick sighed. "You're probably right. But I was hoping so much I'd see Helene."

"I'm sorry," said Kay, "but we won't give up yet. Let's walk around every corridor and into every classroom in the building that's open."

Dick's eagerness was restored as the couple walked from the balcony to the main floor of the building and circled the corridors. Several other masqueraders were walking around, but none wore a costume like Kay's. She looked into various classrooms where couples were seated talking. Not one of the girls proved to be Helene.

"She's not here," Kay said finally. "We may as well go back downstairs."

By this time Dick was thoroughly disappointed. He was silent as he helped Kay down the steps and walked with her through two adjoining corridors without seeing any of the masqueraders. They had just turned a corner

into a third corridor when both were startled at the sight
of a gypsy standing with her back to them. The girl was
alone and she wore a costume which was a duplicate of
Kay's.

"Helene!" Dick cried.

He and Kay rushed forward to speak to her.

CHAPTER XVII

GYPSY TWINS

THE GYPSY masquerader heard Kay and Dick coming and turned quickly. Seeing the other girl in the duplicate costume she stepped back.

"Helene!" Dick cried, grabbing her hand.

"My name is not Helene," the other said icily and pulled her hand away.

"You don't have to pretend," the youth went on. "I'm your brother!"

The girl took another step back. "I have no brother," she said.

Kay put a restraining hand on Dick's arm as he started forward again. "We could be mistaken of course," she said. "We think you are Helene Barbara Caldwell. Are you?"

The other girl did not speak for a few seconds. "What makes you think I am?" she countered.

"Your costume," said Kay. "You posed in it for a magazine cover, didn't you?"

"Who are you?" the girl asked without answering Kay's question.

Kay knew the only way to settle the matter was for all of them to unmask. She made this suggestion. The other gypsy masquerader did not reply at once. But finally she said:

"I guess it can't do any harm."

Each of the three hesitated a moment, waiting for one of the others to be first.

Suddenly Kay laughed. "We're all scared, aren't we?" she said. "Ready! One, two, three!"

The three masks came off at the same moment and the three masqueraders stared at one another in complete amazement.

"Vicki Raponi!" Kay cried.

"Kay Tracey!" the art student exclaimed. "And Bro! What a surprise!"

The youth showed his keen disappointment. "Can you tell me where my sister is?" he asked.

Vicki said she had no idea, but she did have a strange story to tell them. It might help to find the missing girl.

Just that morning a mysterious person had sneaked in to Mr. Raponi's art store without anyone seeing him. He had left a package containing the costume and a note addressed to Vicki.

"It was from Helene," the girl explained. "The note said that she was desperately in need of money and had thought up a scheme to get some. She had read an ad in a newspaper for a gypsy costume."

"That must have been yours, Kay," Dick interrupted and the girl nodded.

"The ad gave Helene an idea," Vicki went on. "There are to be several fine prizes given at the masquerade. She asked me please to wear the gypsy costume to the dance. If it received a prize would I exchange it for money and send the cash to her?"

"The poor girl!" Dick said sympathetically.

"Where did Helene want the money sent?" Kay asked.

Vicki said the girl had given no address. If Helene learned from the newspaper that the gypsy costume had received a prize, she would let Vicki know where to send the money.

"Then you just *have* to win a prize," Kay insisted.

"But how about you?" Vickie said. "Your costume is an exact duplicate and if the costume is chosen, we both deserve a prize."

Hearing this, Kay's brain began to work fast. There were many, many beautiful and original costumes at the masquerade so the gypsy dress, despite its unusual red scarf, stood only an average chance of winning. But suppose the two girls acted as twins! Then they might receive the prize together. She told her idea to the others.

"Wonderful!" Vicki said. "When they have the grand march, you and I will walk side by side."

"Oh, I hope you get a big prize!" Dick said. "For Helene's sake."

Kay related her experience with the Red Devil and asked if he had spoken to Vicki as well.

"No, he hasn't," Vicki replied. "I haven't even seen him."

"Good!" Kay said. "Then maybe we can work together on a scheme to find Helene."

She told Vicki of her suspicions that the man was Tad Bacon and how she wanted to capture him for questioning.

"Oh, I hope you succeed," the art student said. "I'm sure he's back of all Helene's worries."

Vicki was aghast to hear that the man had accused the lovely model of being a thief. She asked Bro how he was getting along and was delighted to learn that he had discovered his first name was Dick.

The boy added enthusiastically, "I just know that

when I meet my sister, my entire memory will be restored."

"I'm sure it will be," the other said kindly.

The group suddenly heard laughter in the adjoining corridor and adjusted their masks. Vicki said she thought that until Tad's capture had been made, perhaps she would stay out of sight and let Kay work alone.

"I came without an escort, and I don't mind missing a few dances. I'll hide somewhere," she offered.

Kay felt this was a wise move too, so they looked around for a room in which Vicki might wait. But each of the rooms on this floor was locked.

"The cafeteria!" Kay said. "It's open and will be the ideal place."

"Where is it?" Vicki asked. She had not attended Carmont High and knew little about the building.

Kay said, "Follow me," and led the way up the dim corridor. At the far end was the darkened entrance to the cafeteria.

"Do you mind waiting here?" Kay asked Vicki.

"Not at all. Anything to get Helene and Dick out of the mess they're in."

Dick murmured his thanks. Then he and Kay went back to the dance floor, so that the Red Devil would know the gypsy girl was still there. He passed the couple in a few minutes and nodded to Kay.

"Fifteen minutes left," he said tersely.

Presently Ronald Earle came onto the floor and claimed Kay as a partner. As they danced off, he said that he had located Chuck.

"He's keen to pull off the stunt," Ronnie reported. "When do you want us to start?"

"Right away," Kay replied.

She told him of having discovered that Vicki Raponi

was there and wearing Helene Caldwell's costume and the reason for it. Ronnie whistled.

"This mystery sure is crowding in," he remarked.

"Chuck's waiting on the first floor corridor for us. I told him I'd get you and we'll fix him up to look more like a real cop. Then you can give him his instructions."

Reaching the doorway, the couple left the dance floor and went upstairs to meet Chuck. When Kay saw him, she burst into laughter and kept on until the tears rolled down her cheeks.

Normally Chuck was a well-dressed boy whose bearing was very straight. He wore an air of dignity as one of the junior class officers.

But now he was dressed in baggy blue trousers, and a coat that looked short-waisted. It had extra long sleeves which covered his hands. The boy had on a small gray derby hat and swung a club in one hand. Around his neck was a whistle on a cord.

Instead of a mask his face was painted almost like a clown's with bright red dots circled on his cheekbones and a dab of white on the tip of his nose, making it appear frostbitten. He wore a small mustache which he was twirling with gusto.

When Kay recovered her composure she wondered how they could ever make Chuck resemble a present day cop. Ronnie steered them into a classroom and said:

"Well, Kay, what do you think?"

Kay studied the policeman's costume. The trousers could be hiked up so they would hang straight. This was done. The coat, she discovered, had a small pad under each shoulder to lift it up. When these were removed the coat would be long-waisted enough.

Next Kay turned the sleeves up to the proper length.

In the dim light the cuffed effect would not be noticed, she was sure.

"We'll have to do something about a hat," Kay said. "Did you see anyone around, Ronnie, wearing one that would pass for a policeman's?"

After a few moments' thought Ronnie recalled having seen a masquerader who was wearing a yachtsman's outfit.

"I don't know who he is," Ronnie said. "But I'll find him and ask to borrow his cap." He went off.

While the others were waiting for him, Chuck scrubbed his face and then Kay gave him instructions about what he was to do. The "policeman" was to wait outside exit number three of the gymnasium. Kay and Ronnie would dance until they found the Red Devil. Then the youth would suggest a change of partners.

"I'll steer Tad toward the exit," Kay said. "Then you be ready."

"I hope everything'll work out all right," Chuck said. He laughed. "I only hope I won't be penalized for impersonating an officer of the law!"

"If you capture a crook, I guess you won't mind," Kay chuckled.

"You're right," agreed Chuck. "It'll be worth taking a chance."

At this moment Ronald returned with the borrowed cap. Chuck put it on. The cap fitted perfectly and looked enough like a police officer's hat for the boy to play the part.

"Well, I guess we're all set," Kay said.

Her pulse was racing as she and Ronald entered the gymnasium and started to dance. They had gone only halfway around the floor when she spotted the Red Devil with—of all people—the duchess!

"This is too good to be true," Kay chortled. "I wish Betty and Wilma could be on hand to see Ethel's face when we capture the Red Devil."

"I do too." Ronnie grinned. "I'm sure her highness won't be exactly delighted!"

He danced near the other couple, and, as planned, asked for an exchange of partners. Ethel's chin and mouth clearly showed that she was thrilled by his request. It proved her popularity!

"Having a nice time?" Ronnie inquired, disguising his voice.

"Oh, wonderful!" Ethel replied. "But such a mob! I don't care for huge crowds, do you? Let's dance toward the corridor and take a walk."

Ronald Earle stifled a laugh. The last thing he wanted to do was stroll in the corridor with Ethel Eaton! Besides, he had to be on hand when the "policeman" tackled her former partner.

"We'll go outside in a minute," he promised.

He kept close to Kay and the Red Devil. Kay was saying to her partner, disguising her voice to make it sound as much like Helene's as possible, "Oh, Tad, do I really have to leave the party so early?"

"Not if you stick around so I can see you all the time," the man replied. "Say, you're a grand dancer."

"You are, too," said Kay, almost hating herself at having to be pleasant to such a heartless individual.

Over his shoulder she could see exit number three looming up. Upon reaching it, Kay pretended to turn her ankle. The Red Devil caught hold of her elbow.

"Oh, dear," she gasped, "I can't dance for a few minutes. Let's go outside."

Followed by her partner, she hobbled into the corridor. Ronnie, having recognized Kay's ruse as the signal for action, led Ethel rapidly to the hallway. A moment later a blue-clad figure emerged suddenly from the shadows.

"A policeman!" Ethel shrilled and scooted away.

Officer Chuck grasped the Red Devil's arm and ordered gruffly, "Come with me!"

"What for?" the masquerader asked vehemently. "I haven't done anything."

"Nevertheless, you're coming with me!"

When the Red Devil tried to pull away, Ronnie jumped forward to Chuck's assistance. Their prisoner was propelled swiftly up the corridor into the darkened cafeteria.

CHAPTER XVIII

THE TRAP

KAY, THE LAST of the group to enter the dark cafeteria, flicked on one of the switches near the doorway and a soft light spread through the room.

The prisoner, whom Ronnie and Chuck had marshaled in, struggled violently. But when Ronnie pulled off the fellow's mask, he quieted down and looked at the boys defiantly.

"Tad Bacon!" Vicki whispered tensely to Kay and Ronnie.

"What's the meaning of this?" the man demanded of Chuck.

Dick stepped forward to take a close look at Bacon. "He's the one who took me away and locked me in the empty house!" the boy cried. "I recognize him even if he was disguised then with a mustache."

"Yes, and he's the same fellow who tied me up," Kay said.

At this moment the prisoner became aware of the two young women dressed exactly alike as gypsies. He muttered something under his breath and covered his eyes with one hand, as if unwilling to believe what he saw. When he recovered his composure, the man looked at

Kay and Vicki again. The girls had by now removed their masks.

"Oh, no! Oh, no!" he cried out, falling back against one of the tables. "You're not Helene!"

"Your game's up, Tad Bacon!" Ronnie said to him, taking off his own mask. "Now tell us what your real name is."

The prisoner did not answer at once. He was obviously trying to pull his wits together and finally succeeded.

"You called me by my right name," he stated defiantly. "So, if you'll let me out of here, I'll go away and not bother you any more."

"What!" Ronnie snorted. "Let a kidnaper go!"

"I'm not a kidnaper and don't say that again," Tad almost shouted, his eyes blazing. "I had a good reason for taking Dick——" The speaker bit his tongue as if he regretted having said this much.

Nevertheless he calmed down and continued, "I *did* have a good reason for taking this boy away. He's a thief and ought to be locked up. I was holding him at that old house so he'd break down and tell me the truth."

"You're lying!" Dick cried. "You never asked me a single question."

Kay, who had purposely remained out of the argument, broke in abruptly. "Where's Helene?" she questioned.

"Why she's—how should I know?" the man flung at Kay.

The import of his first two words was not lost on Kay and she gazed at him steadily. "You're going to do one of two things, Tad Bacon," she said evenly. "Either you take us to Helene or we'll take you to police headquarters."

"Why you—little vixen!" the prisoner shouted. "What right have you to order me around?"

In his anger Tad shook off Ronnie's grip and yanked the red scarf from around Kay's head. He dropped the silk square on the floor and trampled on it.

Immediately Ronnie and Chuck sprang at him and grabbed his arms, while Kay retrieved the scarf.

"You beast!" Vicki Raponi flared. "You're nothing but a scheming trouble-maker, but you won't succeed in frightening Kay Tracey as you did Helene Caldwell. We know you're responsible for her hiding away and you're going to be punished for it. You'd better tell us where she is and do it quickly!"

"You heard what she said," Ronnie added grimly, tightening his hold.

The man who called himself Tad Bacon looked from one to another of the group around him. There was no question but that these young people meant business. Surprisingly, then, he laughed.

"You've got me all wrong," he said, taking on a wheedling tone. "Why, you ought to thank me for protecting Helene. She's a thief——" The speaker turned toward Chuck the policeman. "I shouldn't let you know this but——"

All of a sudden Tad's benign manner changed again. Tearing himself away, he took hold of Chuck and shook the youth violently.

"Why you low-down fraud!" he shouted, staring at the ill-fitting sleeves which once more hung down grotesquely. "You're no policeman. What kind of a joke is this, anyway?"

Kay admitted that Chuck was not an officer of the law, but added that the whole situation was no joke. She reminded Bacon that he had used another assumed name —that of Hamm—when inquiring about the old farmhouse where he had kept Dick a prisoner.

"What of it?" Tad said angrily. "Plenty of people give false names when they're trying to find out about property. I was interested in buying that old place, but I didn't want anybody trailing me to make the sale."

Kay did not believe one word of this story. She told the prisoner that things might go easier for him if he would identify Dick.

"Doesn't he know who he is?" Tad's air of amazement did not convince anyone.

"You know very well he's suffering from amnesia," Kay said sternly.

"All right. His name's Dick Ludlow. Now are you satisfied?" the prisoner cried.

"The name doesn't sound right to me," the boy mused. "Where did I come from?" he asked eagerly.

"From an orphanage. You and your sister both," was the scornful reply. "She puts on pretty airs to cover it up, but I knew your family."

Dick seemed bewildered at this, and Kay and Vicki exchanged glances. They were shocked at Tad Bacon's announcement. But after a moment of thought, Kay was sure the man was not telling the truth and whispered her belief to Vicki, who agreed.

"We're just wasting time," Ronnie spoke up. "Let's take this guy to headquarters. They'll get the truth out of him."

"I'd really rather have him take us to Helene's first," Kay spoke up, and Vicki nodded that this was her choice too.

"Then let's get going!" Chuck urged.

Kay glanced at her watch. In a short time the grand

march would take place and prizes would be announced. Since Helene needed money which a prize might bring, Kay did not want to be the cause of the girl's losing it. When she told this to the others, Ronnie said:

"You go ahead, girls. I'll take care of this fellow."

"I'll stay with you," Chuck offered. "I don't care anything about trying to win a prize."

Dick also insisted upon remaining with the suspect. With the three boys to guard him, there would be no chance of the wily individual escaping.

"All right, then," Kay agreed. "Come on, Vicki."

Just outside the door of the cafeteria stood a snooping figure, dressed as a duchess. Ethel Eaton, curious to know what was going on, had followed the others. She had pushed open the swinging door just far enough so that she would not miss any of the conversation. Her face was red with anger to know she had been dancing unwittingly with a suspect. And for Kay Tracey to have taken him away from her and receive the glory of having him arrested was too much for the jealous girl.

"I'll fix Kay Tracey!" the duchess determined. "I'll see that she looks like a real ragged gypsy when I get through!"

Ethel ran up the hall as fast as her full skirts would permit, her plan of revenge fully formed.

"Besides, because of Kay and those Worth twins, I almost didn't get to this party," Ethel told herself defensively. "I'll make it embarrassing for Kay Tracey all right—and she'll have an audience. I'll get square for the trick those girls played, sewing up my costume!"

Near the door of the gymnasium she was met by an old-time footman. He bowed low.

"And what are madam's wishes now?" he asked sarcastically.

"Oh, Harry," Ethel said to her escort of the evening, "you've got to help me pull a trick."

"Certainly. What is it?"

Ethel whispered in his ear, giggling all the while. Harry nodded his assent, then she dashed off to the room which the decorating committee had used for its head-quarters. After picking up a pair of scissors, Ethel returned to where the footman was waiting.

"There are Kay and Vicki now," she pointed out as the two gypsy girls sauntered toward the refreshment table. "Now, Harry, you just keep them both talking till I give you the high sign to move off."

"Yes, your highness," the boy said with a smirk.

How Ethel reveled in his footman-like obedience! But she became intent a few minutes later when Harry walked up to greet the two gypsies and gallantly poured glasses of punch for them.

Now was the time, Ethel decided. Cautiously she made her way to the trio, and stood behind them. Harry was saying what a splendid party it was, how exciting the band music and how colorful the costumes. And did the gypsies have any guesses as to who might win the prizes?

As the pleasant chatter went on for ten minutes, Ethel was busily snipping stitches here and there among the basted-on ruffles of Kay's skirt. In the crush of people trying to get refreshments, her mischievous work was not noticed.

Finally it was finished. She nodded to Harry, then flew back to the decorating committee's room to return the scissors. At the refreshment table, Kay said:

"Well, I guess we'd better give someone else a chance. Let's go into the gym."

Though Kay had addressed her remark to Vicki,

Harry had thought she meant him and swept her onto the dance floor.

Suddenly Kay tripped. Looking down, she discovered that the bottom ruffle of her dress had come loose in the back and was dragging on the ground. As she leaned over to pick it up, more stitches gave way and one by one six ruffles came off of the foundation skirt.

In a matter of seconds Kay was standing on the dance floor, holding a bunch of ruffles! The plain tan skirt was revealed bare and ugly. Those dancing nearby chuckled at her odd appearance.

Kay was too dismayed to mind the laughter she was causing. At this critical moment, just before the grand march was to begin, her costume was ruined! Almost in tears, she dashed from the dance floor and found Vicki.

"Gracious! What happened to your dress?" the art student cried in dismay.

"I don't know, but what am I going to do?" Kay asked. "We can't march as gypsy twins now."

"Maybe we can," Vicki said hopefully.

A masquerader who might help them had just passed by. A girl was playing the part of an old woman peddler. Strapped around her neck was a tray, heaped with buttons, hairpins, and packages of pins.

"Please, please, may I have some of the pins?" Vicki begged her. "My friend's costume has ripped and we have to do something in a hurry."

The peddler smiled. "Help yourself."

Vicki grabbed two packages of pins and returned to Kay. Taking her by the hand, she said:

"Where can we go to pin you together?"

"In the girls' locker room."

They rushed to it and got to work. As Kay held the ruffles in place, Vicki put in pin after pin. She still had two ruffles to attach when the girls heard the orchestra strike up a martial air announcing that the grand march was about to begin.

"Oh, it's hopeless," Kay said despairingly.

"No it isn't," Vicki said. "Even if we're the last ones in line, we're going to try winning a prize for Helene."

Kay smiled and leaned over to hold on to a large section of ruffle. Vicki's adept fingers worked like lightning. In a very few minutes the ruffles were back in place.

"Oh, how can I ever thank you?" Kay cried. "Unless someone looked carefully, he'd never know these ruffles weren't sewed on."

Running from the locker room, the two gypsies were in plenty of time to join the grand march. Holding their heads high, with their red scarves tied around their chins, the two girls walked side by side. Round and round the gymnasium the long line of masqueraders went.

After what seemed an interminable time, the musicians stopped playing. The marchers stood still and gazed toward the balcony as the head judge arose. After a few remarks about the success of the party and the large sum of money which various charities would receive, he began to announce the prizes.

"I shall start with those receiving honorable mention," he said and called off a list. There were no gypsies on it.

"And now for the prizes which have been so kindly donated by the various business firms in this area," he said pompously.

He awarded luggage, television sets and several articles. The masqueraders came forward and took bows. They would pick up the articles later. Still Kay and Vicki's names had not been mentioned. Finally there was only the grand prize left. Vicki's spirits had sunk, but Kay was still hopeful.

"And now I shall award the tickets for the cruise—our grand prize," the judge said, smiling expansively.

He looked toward the orchestra and there came a sharp roll of the drums. The Carmont High gymnasium was filled with a hush of anticipation.

CHAPTER XIX

A WILD RIDE

"It gives me great pleasure," said the judge, leaning over the balcony and smiling at the throng of masqueraders below him. "It gives me great pleasure——"

"Oh," thought Kay in an agony of suspense. "Why doesn't he hurry up?"

The man paused to take an envelope from his pocket. Holding it up, he continued:

"It gives me great pleasure to announce that the grand prize—a wonderful five-day cruise—has been awarded to the gypsy twins!"

"Kay, we won it!" Vicki Raponi cried ecstatically, her eyes filling with tears.

Kay was almost too choked up to reply. How happy Helene would be!

"Will the gypsy twins please come to the balcony and receive their prize?" the judge requested.

Amid loud hand clapping, the two girls hurried up the stairway and presented themselves to the committee. As the judge held the envelope toward them, Vicki whispered to Kay:

"You take it. You're really the one who won it."

Kay accepted the prize and thanked the judge and the other members of the committee. Vicki did also, giving a graceful curtsy and holding out her ruffled skirt, as though she were on a stage.

"Wait!" said a man's voice behind them.

Turning, Kay and Vicki saw a photographer about to snap their pictures. There was a flash and a click, then the man said he would like to take another with the judge presenting the award to the girls. Kay laughed merrily. She handed the envelope back to the judge and she and Vicki obediently received it a second time, as another bulb flashed.

"Thank you," said the photographer. "This picture will be in the morning paper. Now if you'll just give me your names and addresses——"

As soon as the man had written down the information and left, Kay spoke to the chairman alone, asking if it would be possible to exchange the tickets for cash.

"Perfectly all right," he said.

Happily the two girls returned to the dance floor. Many of their friends rushed up, among them Wilma and Betty. They congratulated the prize winners, then Betty whispered to Kay:

"I was standing near Ethel when the judge made the announcement. You should have seen the duchess's face! She looked as if she'd like to tear you to pieces!"

Kay smiled. Then she in turn whispered to the twins that Tad Bacon was still their prisoner and the boys were guarding him in the cafeteria. The twins' eyes grew large in amazement.

"How exciting!" Betty exclaimed. "Are you going to turn him over to the police?"

"Not right away," Kay replied. "We're going to make him show us where Helene lives first." She explained that the prize was to be given to Helene. "We can tell her tonight!"

"Or in the morning," Betty suggested. "It's a long ride to North Newton if she's there."

Kay agreed that it was, but by talking to Helene maybe the whole mystery could be solved in the next few hours.

"I wish you luck," said Wilma. "But *please* take care of yourself."

"Will you do me a favor?" Kay asked the twins. "Kindly phone my mother and tell her that I will probably be late getting home."

Betty said she would do this and also inform Mrs. Tracey that Kay and Vicki had won first prize. The girls separated, and Kay and Vicki hurried back to the cafeteria.

Tad Bacon was walking back and forth like a caged lion, with three keepers stationed at vantage points watching him closely so that he could not sneak off.

"Anybody we know get the prizes?" Ronald Earle spoke up.

Kay chuckled. "Believe it or not, Vicki and I won first prize for Helene!"

"What!" the three boys cried together and Dick added, "That's swell!"

Tad Bacon stopped pacing and gazed at Kay as she explained to Ronnie and Chuck that it was because she and Vicki were gypsy twins that they had won the prize.

"Let's get started for Helene's home," she urged.

The prisoner's eyes narrowed and his mouth became a straight line. A moment later his expression took on a look of cunning. This was not lost on Kay, who had been watching him closely. She whispered her fears to Ronnie, who promised to take every precaution with the prisoner.

"Let's get going!" he said.

Kay and Vicki went for everyone's coats. As the group left the high school, there were many curious eyes turned in their direction. But the young people marched quickly to Ronnie's car.

"Tad, you sit in the middle of the back seat," the youth directed. "Chuck and Dick, you sit on either side of him. The girls can ride in front with me."

This was not to the prisoner's liking. He objected at once, saying he wanted to ride in the front seat. From this point, he could direct Ronnie better to Helene's house. But both Kay and the youth refused to agree to this.

"You don't trust me, eh?" the man said. "Do you think I'm a fool? Would I jump out of a moving car?"

They did not reply to the questions. Personally they thought Tad Bacon, given a chance, would do exactly that. Ronnie merely said bluntly:

"I'm running this show. You get in the back seat!"

The prisoner shrugged, and with his two guards climbed in and the doors were closed. Ronnie helped Kay into the front, and then Vicki. As Kay moved over to give the other girl more room, she suddenly gave a loud squeal.

"Goodness!" Vicki cried. "What's the matter?"

"Oh, I sat on some of those pins in my costume," Kay replied, with a rueful laugh. She got up, adjusted her skirt, and then sat down gingerly. "There, that's better."

Ronnie climbed in behind the wheel and backed the car out of the parking space.

"Where to?" he asked.

"North Newton," Kay directed, but to her surprise, Tad Bacon spoke up.

"Helene has moved from there. She lives in High Bridge now."

Tad said there were two roads to High Bridge. The shorter one went through Sandwood and out into the country.

"I'll take that one," Ronnie decided.

A smirk of satisfaction crossed the prisoner's face. Dick noticed it and wondered what was going through the man's mind. He determined to watch the fellow like a hawk to make sure nothing happened to spoil the chances of finding his sister.

Reaching the country road, Ronnie put on more speed. Suddenly he cried out, "Ouch! Kay, what have you got in that skirt of yours? It feels like a porcupine."

Kay explained about the pins, saying she suspected Ethel had done it while Harry Blackstone was talking to her and Vicki.

"Ethel, eh? That's just like her," he grunted.

In a few moments Ronnie yelled again and Kay decided she had better remove the pins from her skirt. Opening the glove compartment of the car, she put in all the pins she could reach. Then Kay got up, turned around and kneeled on the seat. Vicki removed the rest. The ruffles were taken off and stuffed into the glove compartment.

"I'll look funny meeting Helene for the first time," Kay remarked. "Half-gypsy, half-ragamuffin."

"Oh, she won't think anything about it," Vicki spoke up. "Helene is such a sweet girl."

"That's why I want to marry her," Tad Bacon suddenly remarked.

At the man's unexpected announcement, an electrified silence fell on the group, until Dick cried out furiously, "You—marry my sister! I'd never let her!"

"I don't know how you can stop me," said the prisoner with suave assurance. "She's promised to marry me as soon as we get a little money together."

Dick sat back, utterly crushed and bewildered. The thought of Helene, his beautiful sister, as the wife of such a man was beyond belief. The fellow ought to be in jail at this very moment for assault and battery and here he was talking about marrying a lovely girl.

Vicki looked at Tad scornfully. "I don't believe for one instant that Helene has promised any such thing," she flared. "She would never marry you!"

Privately Kay felt the same way, but decided to keep silent for a while. Vicki, being a close friend of Helene's, might be able to trip up Bacon if he were lying.

He laughed unpleasantly and said he could see that the others in the car did not understand the situation. Why, Helene had been deceiving people for years.

"What exactly do you mean?" Vicki cried.

"I mean," said the prisoner, "that to all outward appearances Helene Caldwell is an attractive, lovely girl. But little do you know about what she's doing. I've already told you she's a thief, and that her brother here—he's a thief too."

Vicki, Ronnie and Chuck, who had not heard this accusation against Dick before, were stunned. But they recovered in a few seconds and Vicki asked him to explain his statement.

"Well, first, I'll tell you about Dick here. You all think he's lost his memory. Why I can tell you he's just putting on an act. The truth is he's hiding out."

"Why you——" Dick cried out, his eyes blazing. He seized Tad's arm.

"Hold everything!" Chuck advised, reaching over and

patting the other boy's shoulder. "Let's hear what else this man has to say."

Dick became silent, but he continued to regard Tad Bacon angrily.

"After Helene and Dick left the orphanage," the prisoner resumed his story, "they decided a life of crime would be much easier than earning an honest living."

This was too much for Dick. He grabbed hold of the prisoner's shoulders and shook him hard. Once more Chuck leaned over and advised him not to cause a rumpus.

"Take it easy, pal," he cautioned. "A car's no place for a fight."

Dick muttered something but settled back.

"Go on with your story," Chuck told Tad.

"Well, they turned to shoplifting. That's why I came into the picture. For several years I've been covering up for them and even paying money to get them out of trouble.

"But still they kept on, in spite of my kindness. When Dick had his accident in Brantwood, he was on his way to meet Helene. They were going to pull off a really big job."

At once there was an uproar of protest in the car. Vicki Raponi cried, "Why, you despicable man! There's not one grain of truth in what you're saying!"

Kay in her excitement had turned around and knelt on the seat, facing the man. She was about to say something in defense of the girl whom she had never met, when Dick let Tad have it. He lashed out with his fists, striking the fellow first on one side of his face and then the other.

Chuck tried to stop the fight, but could not keep the

infuriated Dick from swinging left and right at the man's jaw.

Unable to ward off the blows, Tad Bacon suddenly arose in the seat. He swung a hard right to Dick's chest. Then leaning forward, he pushed Kay violently against the dashboard. At the same time he reached across Ronnie's shoulder and gave the steering wheel a hard twist.

The next instant the car left the road and bumped crazily down a steep embankment. Vicki screamed. Kay hit her head hard against the windshield and blacked out.

CHAPTER XX

THE LOST PRIZE

WITH little pinwheels dancing crazily before her eyes, Kay Tracey slowly recovered consciousness. She was lying on the ground and someone was holding her wrist.

"You'll be all right in a minute," a voice above her said.

Kay looked up into the eyes of a middle-aged man. He smiled at her kindly, saying he was a doctor.

The girl became aware that bright lights were focused on her and the scene around her. People were milling about and there were several cars lining the road.

"Pretty mean accident," the doctor said. "How'd you come to run off the road at this place? There's not even a curve here."

His words recalled to Kay exactly what had happened. Tad Bacon had yanked the wheel around and caused the accident. In a faint voice she told this to the physician. As her head cleared, Kay asked how her friends were.

"Everybody got banged up a good bit," the doctor reported, "but the boys are all right. They're around here somewhere."

"And how's the other girl?" Kay asked fearfully when she realized he had not mentioned Vicki.

"She's still unconscious but I believe she'll be all right," the doctor said. "We're going to take her to the hospital in an ambulance."

For the first time Kay realized that the bright lights shining on the group were from the headlights of an ambulance parked nearby. On its roof a little red light blinked on and off.

"You're sure Vicki will be all right?" Kay said. "I feel better now. Will you take me to her?"

The doctor helped Kay to her feet and walked with her to the rear of the ambulance. The driver and Ronnie were just lifting a stretcher into the vehicle. Vicki Raponi lay motionless on it, her face chalk white.

"Oh, Vicki!" Kay cried. "I got you into this. If anything should happen to you——"

The doctor laid a hand on Kay's shoulder. "Don't get yourself upset, miss," he advised. "You had a bad crack on your own skull. Take it easy."

He led her off to a little distance and the ambulance pulled away. In a few moments Ronnie joined her and anxiously inquired if she really were all right.

"Yes, I am," Kay assured him. "Honestly."

Ronnie said she must get home as quickly as possible.

"That's a sound idea," the doctor agreed.

"But how?" Kay said. "Your car must be a wreck."

Ronnie smiled ruefully. "Pretty nearly. It's on its side. A wrecking crew will be here any minute."

For the first time Kay noticed that a police car was among those on the road and two troopers were busy looking around.

"They got here soon after the accident," Ronnie explained. "Do you know what caused it?"

"Yes." Kay shuddered. "Tad Bacon made us swerve off the road, didn't he?"

"He sure did, the skunk! He might have killed us all!"

As Kay was about to ask where Tad was, Chuck and Dick walked up to them. Both had large bumps on their foreheads and were very disheveled looking.

"Oh, Kay," said Dick, "I'm so glad you weren't injured. Everything was my fault. Why did I ever have to involve you and your friends in my troubles?"

"Let's not think about that now," said Kay quickly. "Where's Tad Bacon?"

The three boys looked at one another. Finally Chuck owned up that the follow had escaped.

"He was the only one who evidently wasn't stunned," he said. "I guess he had the best seat in the car. Anyway, he knew what he was doing and could protect himself."

"He did just that by ramming into my back," declared Ronnie angrily. "It still hurts."

Chuck said that he and Dick, even though they were dazed, had tried their best to hold on to the prisoner after the car finally had come to a halt. But he had pushed past them and gone out the door of the tilted automobile.

"He shouldn't be too hard to find in that Red Devil's costume," said Kay. "Have you told the police about him?"

The boys assured her that they had. An alarm had been sent out for the fellow but up to the moment Bacon had not been caught. They had barely reported this, when Kay saw one of the troopers walking toward the group.

In his hand he held the Red Devil's costume!

"Where did you find it?" Kay cried.

The trooper said that in searching the area to see if Tad Bacon might be hiding, he had come across the costume.

"Your prisoner must have been fully dressed underneath it," the officer remarked. "He's sly enough to play safe."

"I wonder where he went," Kay mused.

The trooper said they were still looking for him, and Kay, after telling him about Helene Caldwell, urged that the police try to locate her also as quickly as possible. Kay voiced her fear that the missing girl was in more danger now than she had ever been.

"I'll radio your appeal at once to all the cars and town police in this section," the officer promised and walked off to do this.

The wrecking crew arrived and Ronald's battered car was hauled up the embankment. The young people surveyed it sadly. Kay felt particularly bad because she had ridden in it so often to enjoyable parties that she felt as if an old friend had been injured.

As soon as the tow car pulled away with Ronald's automobile, the trooper returned and offered to take the young people to Brantwood. There was not much talking as they rode along. Everyone seemed in low spirits, and each thought what a sorry masquerade it had become —since the evening's gay start so many hours before. Kay was glad when she and Dick reached her own home.

It was three o'clock but lights were on in the Tracey household. Kay was sure her mother must be frantic with worry, wondering where her daughter and Dick were. Mrs. Tracey opened the door for them and surveyed the couple. Her first expression of dismay at their appearance quickly changed to one of tearful joy.

"Kay! Dick!" she cried. "Whatever happened to you?"

Her exclamation must have awakened Cousin Bill for he dashed down the stairway a couple of minutes later.

As he and Mrs. Tracey listened intently to Kay's recital of the evening's adventure, the lawyer's face became very grave.

"That was a risky thing to do, Kay," he declared. "I advise you to stay as far away from Tad Bacon in the future as possible."

"But, Cousin Bill, if I do that, how are we ever going to find Dick's sister for him? Our only clue is through Tad Bacon."

After some argument between the cousins, Mrs. Tracey said that Kay and Dick should get a good night's sleep and think no more about it. They would talk about the whole affair in the morning. Perhaps something could be worked out without Kay running into such danger.

"I'll get some cookies and hot milk and bring them upstairs to you," she offered. "To bed now, both of you, and sleep at least until noon."

Before going to her room, Kay insisted upon telephoning the hospital to see how Vicki Raponi was. To her relief she learned that the girl was conscious now and responding to treatment. It would be necessary for her to remain in the hospital a few days, but only to rest.

"May I come to see her tomorrow?" Kay asked.

The floor nurse who had answered the telephone said she would find out. The woman came back in a few moments and told Kay that it was thought best Miss Raponi should not see anyone until she had returned home.

Kay thanked the nurse and said good-by. She determined to visit Vicki the moment the girl was released from the hospital.

As Kay took off her damaged costume and hung it in the closet, she looked at it with mingled thoughts. It had brought her happiness, excitement, embarrassment, a prize and a close shave with death.

Suddenly she realized that the red scarf was gone. Where had she lost it? Kay tried to remember whether or not she had been wearing it in the car.

"Yes, of course I was," she decided.

Her curiosity getting the better of her, Kay determined to find out if the scarf was still in the car. Going to her mother's room, she telephoned to the all-night towing service. As she held the line, the man in attendance went to look inside Ronald's battered automobile. He came back to report that the red scarf was not there.

"Thank you," Kay said. She hung up and to herself added, "Oh dear, I don't want to lose that scarf. I wonder if it fell off my head when I was carried from the car after the accident."

Her mother, overhearing the conversation, pleaded with her daughter to forget the whole mystery for the time being. Would Kay please get to bed for a sound night's sleep? Then, too, she had had a mean bang on her head, which was all the more reason for resting.

"All right, Mumsy dear," Kay smiled. "I promise to sleep like a top." She kissed Mrs. Tracey good night for the second time and went to her room.

But Kay could not go to sleep. Try as she might to forget the evening's happenings, they paraded before her eyes like scenes from a motion picture. Each episode ended with a vision of the Red Devil. Suddenly a startling thought came to Kay.

"Maybe he took my scarf," she told herself, recalling how he had yanked it off in the school cafeteria.

The girl now recalled the look of cunning which had twice come into Tad Bacon's eyes. While the man could not have exactly foreseen how he was going to escape, no doubt the method he used was what he had in mind all the time.

Upon reaching a certain section of the road, Tad had caused the melee in the car at a time best suited to his own purpose to catch his captors off guard and bring about the accident.

"I'm sure that if he took my scarf," Kay thought, "he'll use it for some sinister purpose."

The girl's heart began to beat quickly as she enumerated all the possibilities. Cousin Bill was right—she would have to proceed with great caution now in working on the mystery.

As this thought haunted her, another one just as disturbing came to the young sleuth. Bouncing out of bed, she turned on her bedside light and rushed to her closet.

Excitedly she reached into the pocket of the gypsy costume where she had tucked the cruise tickets.

They were gone!

CHAPTER XXI

A RAY OF HOPE

THE LOSS of the cruise tickets seemed like the final blow in a long chain of misfortunes for Kay that night.

"Oh, I must get them back!" the girl thought wildly. "They're worth a lot of money!"

Knowing that her mother must be asleep by this time, Kay went silently down the stairway to use the front hall telephone. She dialed State Trooper Headquarters. The officer who answered happened to be the one who had driven her home.

"Miss Tracey!" he exclaimed. "I thought you'd be sound asleep by now."

"I suppose I should be," she said. "But I've just made a dreadful discovery. At the masquerade the other girl who was in the accident and I won two tickets for a cruise. I had them in the pocket of my costume. They're gone!"

"You think they may have dropped out at the scene of the accident?" the trooper asked.

Kay said she hoped this was the case. She also told him about her missing scarf. Would the troopers mind looking at the spot and letting her know if they found them?

"We'll do that immediately," the officer promised. "But don't hold out too much hope. We combed the place pretty thoroughly looking for clues to Tad Bacon. If any of the men had found an envelope or a scarf he would have turned them in."

The girl said she was worried that the finder of the tickets might exchange them for cash first thing in the morning.

"We'll take care of that," the officer promised. "A man will be at the travel bureau where the tickets came from when the place opens."

As Kay wearily climbed the stairs, she met Mrs. Tracey coming from her bedroom.

"Kay, what now?" she scolded mildly.

Her daughter explained and the woman smiled. "You certainly don't leave a stone unturned," she remarked. "Now *please* go back to bed and don't get up again until noontime."

This time Kay obeyed. The girl slept so soundly it was twelve o'clock before she awoke. At first it was hard for her to take stock of her surroundings. Then one by one the events of the evening before came to her.

"I must telephone Trooper Headquarters and find out if the cruise tickets and my scarf have been found," she thought.

Kay dressed quickly and started down the hall. At the top step of the stairway, she met her mother. Mrs. Tracey put a finger to her lips.

"What's the matter?" Kay whispered.

"It's Dick. I'm terribly worried about him. I've sent for the doctor."

Mrs. Tracey took her daughter by the hand, led her into her own bedroom and closed the door. Then she said that while tidying the hall she had heard moanings from the boy's room. Going in, Mrs. Tracey had found him thrashing from side to side and murmuring incoherently.

"I called Dr. Rolfe's office, but learned that he couldn't get here until noontime. Oh, there's the bell now. Probably it's the doctor. Kay, will you let him in, please?"

The girl hurried to the first floor and admitted the physician, who went upstairs at once to Dick's room. Kay and Mrs. Tracey followed him inside.

The youth was quiet now but his face was very pale and his eyes had a burning look in them. Dr. Rolfe took out a thermometer and a stethoscope from his bag. Discreetly the Traceys left the room. Fifteen minutes later the doctor came out and they all went downstairs together.

"Is Dick very ill?" Kay asked him.

"In a way, yes," Dr. Rolfe replied. "But to be honest, I believe it's more mental than physical. The poor boy had a terrific shock last night. This, added to the crack on his head which caused the amnesia such a short time ago, has evidently been too much for him."

Mrs. Tracey looked concerned. "What can we do to help him?" she asked. "Would it be better if he were in a hospital or a sanatorium?"

"No, I don't think that's the answer," the physician answered. "Quiet and rest will be the best things for him." He smiled. "And a good dose of Tracey kindness—the variety you people know how to administer."

After the doctor had left, Kay telephoned police headquarters only to learn that there was no report on the missing persons or articles. Sighing, Kay went to fix a small brunch.

While she was eating it, Mrs. Tracey arranged a tray attractively and put some bouillon and toast on it. Then she added a savory meat ball, some orange gelatin and a glass of milk.

"I'll carry it upstairs," said Kay. "I'd like to talk to Dick if he feels like talking."

She carried the tray to his room and he smiled appreciatively. After propping some pillows up behind him, Kay snapped the supports of the tray into place and set it in front of him.

"Thank you," he murmured. "It looks good. I haven't any appetite, but I'll try to eat some of it."

Kay did not want to weary him but she thought if she could make her conversation interesting enough, perhaps he would eat the food automatically.

"I'm terribly lazy," Dick said suddenly. "I ought to be up helping you."

Kay chuckled. "I just got up myself. And Mother said she was late too. I guess Cousin Bill is the only husky around this place."

By this time the boy had finished the broth and toast. As he put his fork into the meat cake, Kay went on:

"You know, if I had a brother, I'd like him to be just like you, Dick."

The youth looked at her searchingly. "You mean it?" he asked. "When I was a kid, some of the boys used to call me a sissy because I didn't want to fight."

"Dick Ludlow was a fighter last night," said Kay.

"You mean me, of course," said Dick. "I think a fellow should fight when it's necessary, but not just pick a fight. As for that Ludlow business—that's not my name."

Dick was eating now as if he were ravenously hungry. In a few minutes he had finished everything on the tray and Kay asked him if he would like seconds.

"Would you mind terribly?" he asked. "My appetite came back all of a sudden."

Kay, thrilled to hear this, hurried to the first floor and quickly prepared more food. As the boy ate it, he himself brought up the episode of the night before. The girl eagerly discussed it.

"Tad Bacon is bound to be caught fairly soon," Kay prophesied, hoping she had hit upon the truth. "With the police in so many towns looking for him, he can't keep in hiding long."

She told Dick about the missing cruise tickets and her scarf.

"I suspect Tad has them," she said. "I haven't much hope of getting the scarf back. But the police will watch every avenue where the tickets might turn up—travel bureaus, advertisements in newspapers, etc. This will be a good way to track Bacon down."

When Dick finished eating, he declared that he felt quite strong again. He was going to get up. Kay remonstrated with him, wondering what Dr. Rolfe would say to this, but her pleas were useless.

"All right, I'll see you downstairs," she said, picking up the tray and leaving the room.

After she had washed the dishes and put them away, Kay sat down in the living room to plan her next move on the case.

"I just can't let this mystery get the better of me," she told herself.

"And now what is the little sphinx worrying about?" a voice asked, and Cousin Bill strode into the room. "You're taking life entirely too seriously. Better snap out of it or you'll lose those rosy cheeks."

Kay laughed. "I wish I had the wisdom of the sphinx, then I'd know what to do."

"Would a plain old lawyer's advice be any good?" her cousin teased her.

Before Kay had a chance to answer, the front door-bell rang. She opened the door to find Miss Elston standing there.

"Oh, I'm so glad to see you," Kay said cordially. "Please come in."

She introduced Bill Tracey to her math teacher and the three walked into the living room and sat down.

Miss Elston smiled at Kay. "I have news," she said. "The principal of the Rose City school where I used to teach answered my letter almost immediately. I brought it with me. Do read it," she requested, taking the envelope from her purse and handing it to Kay.

"Is it good news?" the girl asked quickly.

"Yes, it is."

"Then I'd like Dick to hear it," Kay said. "He'll be downstairs in a minute."

"I'm here now," the youth said from the doorway and walked in.

He greeted Miss Elston and seated himself near Kay. She explained about the letter, then began to read:

"Dear Miss Elston:
Upon receiving your letter I spoke to one of our teachers who has been here for many years. She vividly recalled the Dick and Helene about whom you were asking. She says their name was Corning——"

"Corning!" Dick interrupted suddenly. "Corning—that's my name!"

In his excitement he jumped from his chair and walked rapidly back and forth across the room. The others smiled happily.

"I'm so glad that at last you've found out," Kay said.

"It's such a relief to know who I am. Dick Corning."
He stopped walking and looked at Miss Elston.

"You said my name reminded you of food. How's
that?"

The teacher reddened. "I hope you're not offended.
I——"

"Oh no," Dick said. "Only I don't get the point."

"You've never heard of corning meat?" Miss Elston
asked. "Of putting it in brine to cure it?"

Dick shook his head. Kay nodded automatically but
her mind was on a more serious subject. Could Tad
Bacon's right name be Corning, she wondered. Had his
warped mind found some sardonic humor in calling
himself Bacon and Hamm to avoid detection?

Was he a relative—a black sheep of the family?

"Please read the rest of the letter," Kay heard Dick
say.

She came out of her daydreaming and went on:

> "*—Immediately I looked in our old records and
> found that Dick and Helene had lived at 654
> Spruce Street. Unfortunately I could not find
> out where they had gone to when they moved
> away from Rose City, but I hope this informa-
> tion will be of help to you. Please call on me if I
> can do anything further.*
>
> "*Very sincerely,*
> "*THOMAS BLACK*"

Kay looked at Dick. "Where did you move to?" she
asked him.

The boy said he could not remember, but the old sad
look had gone from his eyes. He laughingly told how he
was learning a lot about sleuthing from Kay. Right now,
why didn't they ask the telephone company for the

numbers of all the people named Corning within a reasonable area of Brantwood.

"You're getting to be a real sleuth," Kay praised him. "I'll make the request and you do the calling."

The girl was back in a few minutes with the information. In an area of a hundred miles in each direction from Brantwood there were only two families named Corning.

"Oh, one of them must be my family!" Dick cried, taking the paper on which Kay had written down the numbers.

As the youth gave the operator the first number, his voice trembled.

CHAPTER XXII

A REVEALING LETTER

THE FIRST call Dick made to a family named Corning brought him no luck. But his conversation with friendly Mrs. Corning restored the boy's composure. No longer nervous, he gave the operator the other number hopefully. It was in the distant town of Wickcliffe.

"Yes, who is it?" asked a man so suddenly that the boy jumped.

"Why, I—that is—is this the Corning home?" Dick finally managed to stammer.

"Who wants to know?"

"I do. I'm Dick Corning."

There was a long silence at the other end of the wire and the boy began to wonder if the speaker had hung up. But he had heard no click and finally said:

"Hello."

"Who did you say you are?" the unpleasant voice at the other end of the wire asked.

"Dick Corning. Who is this?"

"Never mind. But your folks don't live here any more," the man replied.

Dick's hopes fell. He asked how long ago the family had moved away and where they were.

"I don't know and I don't want to. And I wish people would stop bothering me about them."

"I'm sorry," said Dick. "It's terribly important to me that I find my folks."

"I'd advise you to stop looking," the man rasped. "They're a bad lot. But if you really have to find them, I advise you to start looking in jail."

"In jail!" Dick cried.

"That's what I said," the man answered. "Of course I wouldn't want to be quoted on this, but I've heard people say that they were always thieves. If you're honest, you'd better stay away from them. That's all I can say to you."

Dick put down the phone and returned to the living room. His face was ashen white and he was shaking. As Kay rushed to his side, she asked what had happened. The boy put his head in his hands and began to sob.

"It's true after all," he said brokenly. "The Cornings are thieves!"

The girl was so stunned to hear this she also paled. But as Kay gazed at the innocent looking boy before her, she could not believe he was one of them.

"Dick," she said kindly, "even if someone in your family was not honest, I just know you are."

She told him her suspicions that Tad Bacon's real name possibly was Corning. He might be a relative of Dick's or he might just be using this boy with the same name to cover up his own thievery.

"Suppose you tell us exactly what you heard on the phone," Cousin Bill proposed. At the end of the report, he remarked, "We have no proof that this Corning family is yours. Cheer up, old man. This is a big country and we'll track down every Corning in it."

The lawyer's speech gave the boy renewed hope.

Cousin Bill now told the youth what he had not heard before—that the tires on his jalopy had come from various points in the United States, all a good distance from Brantwood.

"You'll probably find your folks living on a ranch out West," Bill Tracey chuckled. "Right now the men are riding the range and looking forward to the time when you'll get back to help them."

Cousin Bill's good humor was infectious. Kay suggested that perhaps the Cornings owned a plantation in the South and were busy at this moment planting cotton. She began to hum Dixie and the others joined in.

"Or maybe my folks are in the lumber business," Dick said, as the song ended. "But even if they aren't I want to visit the Northwest some time and watch the big trees being felled."

"Tell you what I'll do," Cousin Bill spoke up. "Through a national law association I belong to, it will be easy to contact every Corning family in the areas where your tires came from. I'll begin calling the secretaries in the various cities as soon as I look in my yearbook for the names."

As Bill Tracey started to leave the room, Dick jumped from his chair and stopped him.

"No, you mustn't do that," he remonstrated. "That would be a terrible expense to you. I couldn't let you spend all that money for me."

"Oh, you can pay it back some day," the lawyer said.

To Kay's amazement the youth said he was afraid he might not be able to do this. When he had first come to the Tracey home, Dick had felt that he had a lot of money. Now he was not sure.

"You people have done enough for me," he said. "No,

Mr. Tracey, I just couldn't let you make all those expensive phone calls."

Kay could see that the boy was becoming upset again. Winking at her cousin, she said to Dick:

"I know a much cheaper way to find out about the Cornings, and it will be a lot more fun too."

"How?" Dick said.

Kay said that all the following week there was a school vacation. She and the twins had not planned to do anything special.

"What nicer than to go sleuthing in Rose City?" she said. "There must be former neighbors or friends or even relatives of yours in the city, Dick." Turning to Mr. Tracey Kay added, "How about it, Cousin Bill? May I borrow your car?"

The lawyer laughed. "I thought my convertible belonged to the legal department of this family," he said. "But I can see that it has become a detective's car. All right, you may take it, but see that you come home with the mystery solved!"

Dick's eyes were shining. "May I go along?" he requested.

Kay was stumped for an answer. Actually she did not want him to accompany her and the twins. It was possible that the trip might take two or three days. Moreover, he might hamper the sleuth in her work.

Bill Tracey could read his cousin's thoughts and jumped into the breach. "Dick, have you ever traveled with three girls?" he asked, a broad smile on his face.

"Why no."

"Then I'd advise you not to try it," the lawyer said. He became serious. "Actually, Dick, I think there would be a certain element of danger to the whole project if you go along. It seems pretty evident that it is you and your sister whom your enemies are after. Whenever you're with Kay, at once it involves her."

"I see," Dick said. "All right, I'll stay here. But you'll let me know the minute you learn something, won't you, Kay?"

She promised to get in touch with him the instant she found out anything important. Then Kay went to telephone the twins. Betty was keen for the adventure but Wilma remarked:

> *"The search, tis fraught*
> *With dangers grave——"*

On the extension phone Betty broke in:

> *"But solved by none*
> *Except the brave."*

"Oh, all right, I'll go," Wilma conceded. "But let's stay away from that horrible Mr. Bacon."

The following day the twins came to Kay's house to talk over plans for the trip. Seated in their friend's bedroom, they watched her pack a suitcase for the trip.

"What are all those lumps in the pockets?" Betty laughed. "Your detective kit?"

She arose and went over to examine the lumps.

"What did I tell you?" she cried gleefully, pulling out a flashlight, a magnifying glass and a book entitled *Simple Codes*.

"They may come in handy," Kay defended herself.

Wilma was more interested in a new flannel dress which Kay brought from her closet.

"I never saw that before," she remarked. "It's very pretty."

Kay said she had just received it from a friend of her mother's who lived in New York City. It was known as a cruise dress.

"But I shan't be using it for that," Kay giggled. "And speaking of cruises, I wonder where the tickets are that I lost."

She had heard nothing from the police and was afraid they had already been sold privately to some couple.

"Well, Betty," Wilma spoke up presently, "you and I had better go home and pack our own bags. I suppose Detective Tracey will want to make an early start."

"I'd like to," Kay said. "How about nine o'clock?"

"Okay."

As Kay left her home next morning Dick and Mrs. Tracey waved good-by. They wished her luck and the boy reminded Kay of her promise to phone him the minute she learned anything worth while.

"I'll do it."

It was eleven o'clock when the girls reached Rose City. Kay drove at once to 654 Spruce Street. She hopped from the car and went up the long walk to the old-fashioned house.

A young woman who was spading a flower bed near the long porch greeted her. Kay asked if she could tell her anything about the Corning family who used to live there.

"I'm afraid not," she replied, "but I've heard my cleaning woman mention them. She's inside. I'll get her. Lizzy!" she called through an open window of the living room.

A red haired girl appeared at the screen. Hearing what Kay wanted, she directed her to an aunt named Mrs. Leery who had an apartment at 15 New Street.

"Aunt Mary worked for the Cornings for years," the girl said. "Boy, did she ever love 'em! She said they were the finest people that ever lived and she was heartbroken when they moved away."

What a turnabout report this was, Kay thought! Up to now she had heard nothing but unfavorable stories about the Cornings.

"They couldn't have changed!" the young sleuth thought excitedly. "I was right all the time. Dick and his sister are honest. Somebody is trying to undermine their reputations."

Kay thanked Lizzy for her help and hurried back to the car. The twins exclaimed excitedly over the good news and agreed that someone was deliberately spreading false stories about Dick and Helene.

"But why?" Betty asked angrily.

"That's one thing we have to find out," Kay replied.

"I have a feeling we may be too late," Wilma said drearily.

"Don't talk like that," Betty chided her. "Come on, let's get going."

When they reached the apartment house where Mrs. Leery lived, all three girls went to her door. A plump, round-faced woman with pink complexion and gray hair opened it. At once her gaze became startled. Suddenly she hugged Kay tightly. Then, alternately laughing and crying, she kept mumbling:

"Oh, Helene! Sure an' I knew you'd be comin' to see me someday!"

It was a full minute before Kay could convince Mrs. Leery that she was not Helene Corning. The woman daubed at her eyes, smiling sheepishly through her tears as she berated herself for her mistake.

"Sure and I'm just a foolish old woman," she said. "But I always kept hopin' that Helene Corning or her brother Dick would come to see me. The truth is, I've something very important to tell them."

CHAPTER XXIII

A HIDDEN MESSAGE

"Do COME inside, girls," Mrs. Leery invited. "Sure and my conscience will never rest easy till I tell you what happened."

Kay and the twins smilingly followed her into a cozy, old-fashioned living room. The handmade draperies and cushions showed signs of wear but were still pretty.

"Helene is bound to show up some day," Mrs. Leery began her story. "And then I can give her the lovely box her mother sent me. Mrs. Corning was a dear soul and she never missed sending me presents for Christmas and my birthday and other times too."

The speaker wiped a tear from her eyes. "A short time before her death Mrs. Corning—she died a bit before her husband—sent me a tidy little sum of money in an Oriental box. And bless me, if there wasn't somethin' else in the box that I never found until about six weeks ago.

"One day when I was dustin' it, I stopped to admire the hand carvin'. Suddenly I discovered the box had a false bottom and when I pulled it out there was a whole lot of beautiful jewelry inside."

Out of breath, Mrs. Leery paused for a second, then went on, "Now what would an old woman like me be needin' with such fine jewelry? I decided right off that Helene should have it."

"That's quite a story." Kay smiled. "Helene will appreciate having the jewelry, I'm sure. Mrs. Leery, would you do me a big favor? If Helene should come here, ask her please to get in touch with me or her friend Vicki Raponi. It's very important."

"Sure, and could you be tellin' me why?"

Kay thought it best to reveal everything to Mrs. Leery. During her recital the woman kept twisting her apron and shaking her head in disbelief.

"Oh, this is dreadful! Dreadful!" she cried.

"That sweet, lovely girl—why she never could have done anything dishonest!"

Kay agreed. "So you see why it's so essential that we find her," she said.

Mrs. Leery was quiet for several moments. Then suddenly she arose from her chair, saying she wanted to show the girls something. The woman was gone for a few minutes, then returned with a beautifully carved box. She pulled out the false bottom, revealing rings, bracelets and necklaces.

"Oh, how gorgeous!" Wilma said, going into ecstasies over the gems.

"But they're not all I wanted you to see," Mrs. Leery said.

She laid aside several of the pieces of jewelry, disclosing on the velvet mat below a small folded paper. Mrs. Leery handed it to Kay.

"Since you're a detective, this may help you," she said.

The twins got up and looked over Kay's shoulder to read what was on the paper.

"Dear Thaddeus," it said, *"I am enclosing one hundred dollars for the Star Hill Benevolent*

Home. I will try to persuade Richard to give you some also.

Helen."

"Helen was Mrs. Corning and Richard was her husband," Mrs. Leery explained. "Can you make anything out of the note?"

Kay had to admit that she was unable to, except that very possibly the man who called himself Tad might be the Thaddeus mentioned in the note.

"Did you ever hear the Cornings refer to this Thaddeus or Tad?" the girl asked her.

"Sure and I never did," Mrs. Leery replied.

"Will you please tell us everything you know about the Cornings during the time they lived here and after they left?" Kay requested.

Mrs. Leery said she knew little about the family except that the Cornings had no living relatives by the time they moved to Wickcliffe.

"Wickcliffe!" the girls cried out.

Kay explained why they were so excited at hearing this. Mrs. Leery remarked that it would not surprise her if the old codger who had answered Dick's telephone call at the Corning home there was the children's guardian.

"You know," she told them, "Helene and Dick were only little children when their parents died. I heard that they had a mean old guardian. That was why Helene ran away from home. She couldn't bear it any longer."

Here was news, indeed! Kay instantly decided upon her next move.

"Girls," she said, "we're off for Wickcliffe!"

"Well bless you all," said Mrs. Leery as the girls stood up to leave. "I hope and pray that everything will turn out all right for my wee bairns. Tell them to come and see me."

Despite the gravity of the situation, Kay had to smile. Dick was far from being a "wee bairn" and his sister was even older! Nevertheless Kay was touched by the woman's love and loyalty toward the brother and sister whom she had known so many years before.

The girls said good-by and left the house. Mrs. Leery waved and threw kisses to them from her front window as they got into the car and drove off.

"Now what do we do?" Betty asked. "Brave the lion in the Corning homestead?"

"If he is Helene's and Dick's guardian, and he's not honest," Kay replied, "I'm sure we won't learn much from him. I have another idea—to find out what was in Mr. Corning's will."

"How can you do that?" Wilma asked.

"By having Cousin Bill call up the courthouse and make arrangements for me to read the will," Kay chuckled.

"Well, everybody there will be out to lunch," said Betty, "and that's just where we should be. What say we stop some place and you can telephone your cousin from there?"

Kay agreed and presently she pulled up in front of an attractive highway tearoom. Kay went at once to telephone and fortunately found Bill Tracey at his office.

"Well, you certainly didn't waste any time," he praised his cousin when she finished her story. "You've picked up a couple of very valuable clues. I'll get permission at once for you to read Mr. Corning's will. By the time you reach Wickcliffe, it should be out of the files."

"Cousin Bill," Kay said, "will you please tell Dick what I found out from Mrs. Leery?"

"I'll call the house right away," the lawyer promised. "It may help to restore more of Dick's memory."

"That's just what I'm hoping," said Kay excitedly.

The girls ate luncheon and during the drive to Wickcliffe they discussed the case from every angle. Wilma was fearful that Helene's and Dick's guardian had been stealing money from the estate for many years and that there might not be much of it left.

"I can't get it out of my head that the Benevolent Home somehow is involved in the mystery," Kay said. "You remember Tad Bacon told that army man's wife he was thinking of buying the old Stone property."

"You mean to move the Benevolent Home there?" Betty asked.

"Possibly," Kay responded.

"Tad Bacon is anything but a benevolent person!" Betty said indignantly. "I'll bet the whole thing is a phony!"

"I agree," said Kay. "Maybe after I read Mr. Corning's will we'll know more about it."

At the Wickcliffe courthouse Kay was graciously received by a woman clerk who said Bill Tracey had called and arranged for the girl to read the Corning will. She had it ready.

Kay sat down at a table and began to pore through the many sheets. The twins walked up and down watching as Kay's finger ran along the printed lines. A few times the girl murmured and turned back to former pages. Finally she folded the papers and returned the will to the clerk.

"Well," said Betty, hurrying to her side, "what did it say? Is it as big a mystery as we suspected?"

"It's all of that," said Kay. "It's imperative that we do something at once. We must find three people—Helene, Thaddeus Corning and a man named John Snead. There's not a minute to lose!"

CHAPTER XXIV

CAPTURED!

THE THREE girls left the courthouse and Kay remained in deep thought. Betty could not stand the tension any longer.

"Don't we rate knowing what's in that will?" she demanded.

"Of course," said Kay. "Please forgive me. I was trying to figure out our next move. The story in a nutshell is this: Mrs. Corning died a short time before her husband and left everything to him. But listen to this—Mr. Corning divided his money into approximately three equal parts. Helene was to get about a third of it when she became of age. Dick will get his share when he's twenty-one. And the other third, a large amount of cash, was left to the Star Hill Benevolent Home!"

"And if that Home *is* a phony," said Betty, "Thaddeus Corning is going to make off with the bequest."

"How awful!" Wilma murmured.

"It's even worse than that," said Kay. "The date for the money to be given to the Home is tomorrow!"

The twins were dumfounded. "You mean," said Wilma, "that unless we stop this man, it may be too late?"

"Exactly," Kay replied. "If the whole thing is a hoax,

he has probably forged a lot of papers to make the Home seem authentic. It wouldn't surprise me if these were the papers Dick Corning had on him when he was knocked out in his jalopy."

"Maybe," said Wilma. "But it's just possible, Kay, that the whole thing is aboveboard and we'd be wasting our time trying to find Corning and Snead."

"There's one thing I haven't told you," the young sleuth said. "Unless the head of the Benevolent Home can prove that it is a going concern and in sound financial condition, then the money is to go to Helene and Dick."

Betty whistled and Wilma groaned. It now seemed pretty evident that Tad Bacon was indeed Thaddeus Corning. He had been deliberately keeping Helene and Dick away until after he could get the money for the Home and abscond with it.

"But how are we going to prove all this?" Wilma argued. "And where are we going to find these people?"

"We're going out to the Corning House," said Kay. "If nobody's around, we'll spy on the place."

"It's a large order before tomorrow," said Betty, "but I'm with you. Let's go!"

"First I must call Cousin Bill," Kay told the twins. "I'll ask him to find out what he can about the Star Hill Benevolent Home. And I'll ask him to telephone Dick and tell him everything up to date."

While Kay stepped into a store to use the telephone, Betty and Wilma went for the car. By the time Betty maneuvered it out of the parking lot behind the courthouse and turned the corner, Kay was waiting for them at the curb.

"You drive, Betty," she said, opening the door and squeezing in beside Wilma.

A traffic cop gave them directions to the old Corning homestead. It was a couple of miles out of town and proved to be a fairly large estate. As the girls looked at it, they were surprised, yet disappointed. The place indicated that the Corning family once had great means, but the estate had been allowed to run down so that now it was overgrown and shabby.

As Betty started to turn in the long, rutted lane, Kay said she thought they had better not drive up to the house. They could leave the car on the road and stroll in casually, as if they were merely looking the place over. Betty backed around and parked, then the three girls hopped out.

It was late afternoon by this time and Wilma declared that the long shadows cast by the trees gave the place a spooky atmosphere.

"Oh, don't start that," Betty scolded her. "You always manage to give me the shivers when we work on a mystery."

Wilma said no more, but Kay smiled. She too sensed that there was a sinister feeling about the old estate.

Reaching the front door, Kay lifted the heavy knocker. She could hear its thud resound through what was apparently a large hall. Several minutes later she heard footsteps. From behind the massive door a man's high cackling voice called:

"Who's there?"

"I'd like to find out something about the Cornings," Kay replied, using a tone as sweet and wheedling as she could.

"Well, you're wasting your time," the man answered. "I don't know anything about them. Go away!"

"Have you any idea where they live now?" Kay pressed.

"No, and don't bother me," the grumpy speaker said insistently.

Kay and the twins looked at one another. Was this person faking or did he mean what he said? As Kay debated what to do next, the old man shouted sternly:

"Go away, I tell you!"

The girls could hear him plodding back along the hall. Knowing it was hopeless to find out anything from him, they turned away and walked down the driveway.

"The mean old thing!" Wilma said. "To think he wouldn't even open the door—just as if we were a lot of burglars!"

As they reached the car, Kay noticed a bus coming up the road. As she started off, the girl stayed far to the right. She had gone only about fifty yards when she glanced into her rear view mirror. The bus had stopped in front of the Corning estate! Kay slowed to a snail's pace and suddenly cried out:

"Girls! Look!"

The twins turned around in time to see a woman step from the bus. Over her head was a red scarf!

"I'll bet that's mine!" Kay exclaimed.

As the woman scooted up the driveway, Wilma said, "Maybe it's Helene Corning!"

"I doubt it," said Kay. "I'm sure Vicki Raponi still has Helene's costume."

"Then who is that woman?" Betty demanded.

"I don't know, but we're going to find out!" Kay answered.

She had already turned off the motor and was getting out. The twins followed quickly.

It had grown even darker since their first trip to the house and it was easy for the girls to melt into the shadows of the trees. By the time they reached the house, lights were twinkling in one of the first floor rooms. Automatically their footsteps took this direction.

One of the windows was open and the three girls posted themselves just below it. By stretching a little and standing on tiptoe, Kay could see two men in the room. One was Tad Bacon! As she listened, he called the other man John Snead!

A moment later the woman wearing the red scarf entered the room. Tad Bacon's eyes blazed.

"Maisie!" he shouted. "I told you not to wear that scarf. Do you want to give everything away?"

The woman swaggered toward him. Tossing her head, she said, "Dear brother, what have we got to be afraid of now? By tomorrow morning we'll be out of this place."

"That's what we hope, if you don't spoil everything, you dumbbell!" Tad said, shaking her. "Kay Tracey's a slick one. She may be in Wickcliffe right now."

"Aw, you've got those forged papers from Dick," Maisie said in a sneering tone. "Even if she didn't pay any attention to that warning you left about Dick being a thief, what can Kay Tracey do? We're sittin' pretty." She laughed unpleasantly. "Nobody's as smart as you, Tad, or should I call you Thaddeus the Great?"

Wilma tugged at Kay, urging her to leave, but Kay felt more would be revealed if they stayed to listen.

"It was real shrewd of you," Maisie went on, "to steal the cruise tickets, sell them, and put the money toward our passage to South America."

"Will you shut up?" Tad screamed at her.

This time the woman became quiet. Kay was sure that now the girls had heard everything necessary to bring about the arrest of these people. She beckoned to the twins and they started away from the house together.

But at that very second, they heard a second-floor

window being opened. Before they could dive out of sight, a man looked down at them.

"Spies!" he shouted at the top of his voice.

The three girls started running pell-mell down the driveway. They had not gone far when they saw a man coming toward them.

"Halt!" he ordered.

The girls had no idea of halting. Instead, they turned around and started running first in one direction, then another. But their escape was cut off from every route.

John Snead and Tad Bacon, as well as Maisie and the man from the second floor raced from the house and surrounded the group. Under threats, Kay and the twins were marched inside. Tad Bacon's face became livid.

"This time there'll be no getting away for you, Kay Tracey!" he gloated.

CHAPTER XXV

A HAPPY REUNION

IN THE Tracey home next morning at ten o'clock Dick Corning was frantically dialing a telephone number. He was using the second floor telephone and hoped he could put his call through before Mrs. Tracey might hear him. What he had to say would certainly worry her.

"Hello, Ronnie? This is Dick. Can you come right over? My amnesia's gone and I remember a lot of things. I'm sure Kay and the twins are in great danger but Mrs. Tracey mustn't know it. We must go after them as quickly as possible." Dick paused, then added, "Good. I'll get ready!"

He hung up, his face tense with apprehension. Within ten minutes Ronald pulled up in front of the Tracey house. As casually as possible he went inside and told Kay's mother he had come to see if Dick would like to go out with him. She smiled, saying she thought it would do him good.

The boys tried to make their leave-taking seem natural, but Dick's eyes burned with excitement. As soon as the boys were out of sight of the house, he directed his companion toward Wickcliffe. Ronnie drove as fast as the speed limit would permit while Dick told him the story of his life.

His parents had died when he and Helene were young. A very strict guardian by the name of John Snead had been appointed to take care of them. He and his wife had moved into the Corning home.

"Mrs. Snead was very nice," said Dick. "But when she died about six years ago, things got pretty bad. Helene couldn't stand it after a while and finally ran away from home. After that Mr. Snead wasn't so bad, but he would never tell me anything about my parents' affairs.

"When Helene was twenty-one, I asked Mr. Snead if he wasn't going to try to find her. Surely she must have some money coming to her. He had little to say except that finding Helene was impossible. He said detectives had been looking and had concluded she probably was no longer living."

Ronnie whistled in surprise.

"That just about killed me," Dick went on. "Mr. Snead became quiet and mysterious. He wrote long letters, but I never saw the addresses.

"Then one day a phone message came for me. It was from Helene! She was calling from Carmont. She told me her address but said not to let Mr. Snead know what it was.

"I tried to talk to her some more but just then my guardian came into the room. He demanded to know whom I was talking to. I just couldn't tell him so I said it was a wrong number."

"When was that?" Ronnie asked.

"About a month ago," Dick replied. "It was not long afterward that I began to grow suspicious of Mr. Snead. I suggested that my folks must have left a lot of money but the way we had lived for years, letting the house and the grounds run down, wouldn't indicate this.

"He told me that I needn't fool myself. There was

very little money in the estate, but when I was twenty-one I would get my share. Helene's was being held for her. As soon as she showed up, she could have it."

Ronnie raised his eyebrows. "You didn't believe that, did you?"

"I guess I did," Dick said sadly. "Then I foolishly blurted out that I knew where Helene was and I was going to get her at once. Mr. Snead didn't say anything but I could see that he didn't like it. This made me more suspicious than ever."

Ronnie slowed down to negotiate a sharp curve. "Then what did you do?"

"That night after he had gone to bed, I picked the lock on his desk to hunt for papers. I was sure there would be a copy of my father's will and I wanted to find out what it said. I found out all right—and something else too! My father had left one-third of his estate in cash to a benevolent home. And more papers in the desk proved it was a phony.

"I decided then and there to find Helene and together we would have Mr. Snead and his friend Thaddeus Corning arrested. Well, Ronnie, you know what happened after that."

"Wow! What a story!" Ronald exclaimed. "It's a good thing you got your memory back. Let's hope we find the girls before something happens to them."

Dick said it was his hunch they would find Kay and the twins at his home. It was not until mid-afternoon that they reached there.

"There's no sign of life around here," Ronnie remarked as they pulled up to the front door of the house.

Dick used the knocker. When there was no response, he told of a secret entrance to the house. Ronnie followed him to the rear, where Dick parted some bushes and slid back a panel in the foundation. The two boys crawled through to the cellar.

"This way," he directed.

Excitedly he led the way to the stairs which went up to the kitchen. Food and unwashed dishes gave evidence of a hasty exit by the occupants of the house.

"Listen!" Ronnie ordered.

From somewhere above them they could hear a knocking sound.

"We'd better see what it is. You lead the way, Dick."

As they raced up the front stairway, the noise became louder. Finally they traced it to the attic. But when they burst inside, no one was in sight.

"It must have come from the secret attic!" Dick cried.

Racing across the floor, he began working at one of the panels in the woodwork. A moment later he had pushed it downward.

"Kay! Wilma! Betty!" the boys cried together.

The three prisoners staggered out to the main attic. Weak from hunger and fright, they could not speak above whispers. But they expressed amazement that their rescuers had found them.

"My memory is restored!" Dick exclaimed. "That's why Ronnie and I are here."

The boys half-carried Kay and the twins down to the kitchen. There they made the girls sit in chairs while they hustled up some food left in the pantry. After eating a good meal, they felt strong again and their voices returned.

"We still have work ahead of us," Kay said. "Dick, do you know what was in your father's will?"

When the boy replied in the affirmative, she quickly added, "By this time those awful men and that woman

Maisie are on their way to South America with money that rightfully belongs to you. We must call the police and stop them!"

Ronnie offered to do this. While he was making the report, Dick said he never could thank Kay and the twins enough for all they had done for him.

"Now if I could only find Helene, everything would be perfect," he said. "I wonder if she's still at that address I had."

Kay said she was sure Thaddeus Corning, who had gone under the name of Tad Bacon, had frightened Helene into hiding. In fact, he had said as much.

Before imprisoning the three girls in the attic, he had bragged of his dishonest exploits. He and Maisie with Snead's help had found it "advisable" to keep Helene Corning from receiving her inheritance until after the men had been given the money for the phony benevolent home.

"But he did drop a piece of paper with a telephone number on it," Kay said. "I picked it up when he wasn't looking." She took it from her skirt pocket. "I think, Dick, that if you call this number and ask for Helene Caldwell, you'll find her."

Overjoyed, the youth went to the telephone. In a few moments he was talking to his sister. Quickly he told her the whole story, asking if she would come there as soon as possible. She promised to do so, adding that she would like to thank her benefactor in person.

"I hear Kay Tracey looks like me," she said. "If she hadn't been able to masquerade in my place, this mystery probably never would have been solved."

Dick agreed wholeheartedly, but reminded his sister what awful chances the young sleuth had taken in order to help them. Kay blushed.

"It was great fun helping you both," she said warmly after he had hung up.

While they were waiting for Helene, word came from the police that Tad, his sister and their accomplices had been captured at a South American line's pier in New York City. They had confessed to everything, even admitting they had stolen a substantial sum of money from the estate.

When it looked as if Tad's scheme might be foiled at the time Dick started out to find his sister, the man had followed him, waylaid the boy and taken the papers. Dick's amnesia had worked in perfectly—but not long enough!

It took Helene Corning nearly three hours to reach her old home. In the meantime, Kay called Vicki Raponi, who had completely recovered from the accident. Vicki, jubilant at the good news, hurried over and joined the other young people.

During all this time Kay and the twins worked like beavers to tidy and dust the main rooms on the first floor and then tackled Dick's and Helene's bedrooms. Ronnie went to town with a grocery list so that the refrigerator and pantry shelves might be well stocked.

The work had just been completed when lovely Helene Corning drove up in a taxi. She hugged and kissed her brother until he was red from embarrassment.

"Please let me introduce our new friends," he begged finally.

Helene, having embraced Vicki joyfully, greeted the others warmly and, with tears in her eyes, thanked them profusely for all they had done. Kay in turn told her how Dick and Ronnie had rescued them from the attic prison.

"So I guess we're even." She laughed.

"There's just one thing I regret," Helene said. "I wish Tad wasn't a relative of ours. He's a disgrace to the Corning name!"

"He's not a relative!" cried Kay.

The young detective told how she and the Worths had learned from Tad that he had posed as a distant cousin to play on the sympathy of Mr. and Mrs. Corning and eventually get part of their money.

"That's wonderful news!" Helene almost wept in relief.

Kay, thinking sister and brother would like to enjoy their reunion alone, said that she and her Brantwood friends must leave. But Dick would not hear of this and told his sister of the well-stocked larder.

"Indeed, you must stay and help us celebrate our homecoming," Helene argued and finally the others accepted.

What a gay dinner it was! And how different from the staid, silent affairs with Mr. Snead, Dick revealed. Helene insisted upon hearing every detail of the case. She herself confessed that Tad had frightened her out of her wits by lying to her that Dick was wanted for thefts which he said the boy had committed.

"How dreadful!" Wilma cried. "He's a wicked person. Why he even telephoned Vicki and tried to make us think you had drowned!"

"So that's what his call was about!" Helene remarked. "He wouldn't let me phone but I sneaked a call in later."

"One thing puzzles me," Betty spoke up. "How did you get the gypsy costume to Mr. Raponi's shop, Helene?"

"I asked a man to leave it there. And speaking of that costume, Kay, since yours is ruined, I want you to take mine."

"I'd love to have it," said Kay, "especially the scarf. It was the secret of the red scarf that started and ended this delightful mystery and"—she paused to smile at the two Cornings—"brought me two wonderful new friends."

If you enjoyed this story, you'll want to read others about Kay Tracey, America's favorite teen-age detective, and her friends, Wilma and Betty. Here are only a few of the titles in this thrilling series. Your bookseller has them. Watch for the new books to be added periodically.

THE MANSION OF SECRETS
Kay and a sinister intruder match wits in a quest for treasure.

THE SIX FINGERED GLOVE MYSTERY
Kay saves a famous actress from a strange threat.

THE SACRED FEATHER
Kay, with Wilma and Betty, unravels a secret of ancient Egypt.

IN THE SUNKEN GARDEN
Kay puts on dancing slippers to solve a mystery.

THE MYSTERIOUS NEIGHBORS
Kay solves the riddle of the river racketeers.

WHEN THE KEY TURNED
Danger follows Kay as she searches for a priceless violin.

THE SECRET AT THE WINDMILL
The teen-age detective outwits a scheming guardian.

THE MURMURING PORTRAIT
Kay thwarts the evil plans of a weird gypsy.

THE LONE FOOTPRINT
Mystery and danger plague Kay and her friends on a vacation.

THE DOUBLE DISGUISE
Kay unmasks a team of clever jewel thieves.

THE MESSAGE IN THE SAND DUNES
Kay's search for buried treasure leads to adventure and danger.

THE CRIMSON BRIER BUSH
Kay finds the missing clue and outwits the mysterious stranger.

THE GREEN CAMEO MYSTERY
A Chinese puzzle confronts Kay in her hunt for Lotus Wong.

THE STRANGE ECHO
Spooky sounds in the hills beckon Kay on a dangerous mission.

THE SECRET OF THE RED SCARF
Kay's striking resemblance to another draws her into a baffling case.